Tye Watkins in

Last of the War Chiefs

Book 13 of the Tye Watkins Series

Books in Tye Watkins Series

Book #1: Border Trouble

Book #2: The Crossing

Book #3: Yancey

Book #4: The Desperate Trail Kill

Book #5: Drums Along the Border

Book #6: Rack to the Rockies

Book #7: Second Chance

Book #8: Yahzie

Book #9: U.S. Marshal

Book #10: A reason to

Book #11: El Diablo

Book #12: Vendetta

Book #13 Last of the Warchiefs

Mountain Man Series

Book #1: Mountain Man-The Beginning

Dedication: To all those who so many years ago blazed the trail with their courage and sacrifice during the early days of the west so we could have the freedom we have now. This is your great, great parent's story, many of whom lost their lives in the struggle.

Authors Discovery

Odessa, Texas

ISNB#   978-0-9971107-4-6

Cover Concept by Michael McMillan

Authors Note

Around 1873 most of the buffalo who had roamed the Great Plains by the millions were almost gone, killed by the hide hunters. This devastated the plains tribes since the buffalo were their main source of food, clothing, tools and hides for shelter. Most tribes facing starvation were forced to surrender to the army and be placed on reservations.

Most branches of the Comanche, who were known as "lord of the Plains," surrendered and placed on reservations. Quanah Parker, leader of the fiercest of the branches, the Quahada's, did not surrender, and led by Quanah traveled south to the Texas panhandle. There they found a huge canyon southeast of present-day Amarillo which is now named the Palo Duro Canyon. This canyon was approximately 120 miles long and 20 miles wide in places. The walls were steep and some places over 800 feet high.

The Quahada's found buffalo and deer along with other game plus plenty of water. This was the perfect place for them to camp. There was limited places that could be accessed to the canyon floor and could be defended easily. It was the perfect place for them to use as a base to raid the surrounding area and all the way down to Mexico and Fort Clark in South Texas near present day Del Rio.

There were many famous war chiefs of the various tribes: Crazy Horse and Red Cloud of the Ogala Sioux, Black Kettle of the Cheyenne, Geronimo and Cochise of the Apache tribes. But probably the man who killed more settlers and soldiers during the period between 1872 until his surrender in June of 1875 was Quanah Parker. The vary mention of Quanah Parker would result in panic all across the Texas Plains and South Texas.

Quanah continued their raiding until The Red River War in 1874-75. Federal troops under the command of Ranald McKenzie invaded the stronghold of the Quahada in the canyon killing some of the warriors. The most hurt put on the tribe was McKenzie killing over 1400 of their ponies. Continued pressure by patrols being everywhere the Quahada went finally led to Quanah surrendering in June 1875 and placed on the reservation at Ft. Sill, Oklahoma.

This story takes place at the height of the raids the Quahada were committing south of the canyon all the way to Mexico.

The Last of The Warchiefs

BY

GARY MCMILLAN

Chapter One

Second Lieutenant James Booker sat on his mount at the head of the twelve-man patrol he was leading. The patrol was about a quarter mile from the canyon that dropped off to where the Pecos River flowed into the Rio Grande. He was waiting on his scout he had sent ahead to see if the canyon was clear of trouble. Sitting on his horse beside him was First Sergeant Arnold who was the only real veteran with him on this patrol besides the scout. He looked to the Sergeant for advice unlike some other Lieutenants did that he had heard about. There had not been any reported trouble as of yet concerning the Comanche but reports from friendly Apache were reporting it was coming.

"What do you think of the reports of the Comanche coming down this far south, Sergeant?

Absher spit a wad of tobacco out and wiped his mouth with the sleeve of his damnable wool shirt. "Never know Sir. About year and half ago we and the Apache beat the Comanche in a big battle and sent them hightailing back north where they come from."

"What do you mean, you and the Apache?"

"It's a long story Sir. Yahzie, a war chief one of the branches of the Apache tribes along the Border, raised all kinds of hell for a while till Tye put him in his place and believe it or not they became friends. Well, I was on patrol with Captain McClellan checking reports from Ft. Davis that the Comanche were moving south to raid into Mexico looking for Apache horses and women and lo and behold we ran smack into Yahzie. Now, one of the agreements that Yahzie and Tye had was he was to stay out of the Mexico side of the Border. He was not with a bunch of his friends and wanted to talk so McClellan and me, so we had a pow-wow with him. Said he was looking for sign of the Comanche also. While we were talking, one of his braves rode in on an exhausted pony saying a large band of

Comanche were making camp a ways up the Rio Grande apparently trying to find a way to get across the river into Mexico."

"To make a long story short, Sir, between Yahzie and his Apaches and the U.S. Calvary we ambushed the Comanche and sent their butts back where they come from with a lot less men than they come down with."

The story ended when one of his men in the back of the small column screaming Indians! Indians! Looking back Booker saw about fifty warriors charging toward them. He shouted, "Follow me," and the patrol was racing their horses toward the canyon in hopes of crossing the small bridge at the bottom of the canyon over the Pecos and reach the top of the other side of the canyon.

His scout came out of the canyon at a full gallop just before they reached the canyon rim. Booker held up his hand to halt the patrol and looking over his shoulder he saw the warriors were less than a quarter mile behind them and closing fast.

"There about thirty Comanche about a mile of the other side of the canyon and coming fast, Sir" the scout shouted. "Onliest chance we have is to make the other side and fort up in an abandoned homestead I saw."

Booker stood up in his stirrups and shouted, "Follow me," and he took off with the scout at an all-out run down the canyon and across the small bridge over the Pecos and up the other side. Racing over the crest the scout pointed to his right where the home stood. Booker headed toward it and saw the on-coming Comanche about four hundred yards away. The troopers had their mounts on their haunches sliding to a stop and everyone was off their mounts before stopping completely.

"Find a place that offers some protection and hunker down," Booker shouted. He always wondered how he would react when his first action came. He was pleased that he was as calm as he was. "Grab your Spenser's and canteens from your mounts. Private Mason and Private O'Kieth, take the horses behind the homestead." Looking around as he and four of the men went inside the home, he was suddenly optimistic of their chances. The land dropped off behind them into the Pecos and fell off into the Rio Grande on their right. The cliffs walls were forty or fifty feet high. That left only the front and left to defend. He quickly had four men get behind the three-foot rock wall on the left and had four men behind the wall in front. He kept the scout inside with him along with Sergeant Arnold, and Private Fuller. He left Mason and O'Kieth with the valuable responsibility to hold the horses behind the home. With the three men on the wall facing towards the oncoming Indians and with his self, Fuller and Arnold gave them six rifles guarding the front.

The Comanche that were behind them came out of the canyon in an all-out run and were past the homestead before they realized the soldiers were there. Halting their mount and turning to face the soldiers they charged. Being only fifty or so yards away Booker gave the order to fire. Eleven rifles fired as one and there not many misses. This was quickly followed by a couple rounds from the single action colt revolvers the soldiers carried on their hip and several more ponies were empty of their riders. The remaining braves turned away to meet the bunch that were now coming up from the south. They gathered about three hundred yards away and circled a warrior on a solid black pony.

Booker, knowing that Private Fuller was an excellent marksman, called him to the window where he was. "See the warrior on the black horse?"

"Yes Sir."

"Knock him off that damn horse."

Fuller braced his left arm on the base of the window to steady himself and took aim. He allowed for the distance, aiming slightly over the man's head. He stroked the trigger but the brave on the black horse moved at that instant. The warrior that was in front of where the brave on the black horse was blown backwards off his pony. The soldiers hollered their approval of the shot as the warriors jerked their mounts around rode farther away before stopping and facing the soldiers.

The brave on the black horse was none other than the "she-bear of the Comanche," Quanah himself. He was leery of the situation with the soldiers as well protected as they were. It reminded him of the fight he was involved in at Adobe Walls several months earlier when a few white hide hunters held off about 500 or so warriors because of the protection they had and the accuracy of their rifles. He did not think these men had the rifles that shoot as far (Sharps fifty caliber) but he didn't want to lose men unnecessarily either. He called a council with two of the older warriors with him, Little Bear and Broken Hand.

"You were with me at the fight with Buffalo hunters at the place the white men call Adobe Walls. This place reminds me of the fight. They are behind walls as they were there but do not have the big guns the hunters have but they are accurate as you saw when they shot our brother from a long distance a few minutes ago. We need to make a plan to kill them without losing more warriors.

"You got plan," Broken Hand asked?

"Maybe," Quanah replied. "When it is dark tonight Broken Hand and me will take some warriors and go south on foot till we reach the place where road drops into the next small canyon. Little Bear, you take all the others and all the horses and go back past the soldiers making plenty noise so they will believe we all have left. Release arrows as you pass them and then lay low on your pony's backs." Both men nodded their head in agreement. Seeing this, Quanah said, "We will do this. Little Bear, you have to make the bluecoats believe we have left."

Little Bear nodded. "We make them think whole Comanche nation riding by," and smiled.

Lt. Booker told Pvt. Fuller to take up the men's canteens after letting them have a drink. You will be responsible for rationing the water. We may be here awhile, and I want to make sure we have water. I know the Pecos and Rio Grande are below us but I figure the Comanche will have someone watching. Fuller saluted and left and was back within minutes with an arm full of canteens.

He turned to his Seminole scout. "Mr. Bowlegs, why haven't they attacked by now? The sun will be down in little over an hour. They have us out numbered at least five or six to one."

"Been thinking on that Sir. Thinking that warrior was bigger than most Comanche. Had single eagle feather and I have heard Quanah wears a single feather. He was on a black pony that reports say he always rides. Thinking Sir that if'n that be Quanah himself, he is smart and knows we are in a good defensive position, and he could over run us but he would lose a lot of warriors.

"My God!" Booker exclaimed. He walked to the window and looked at the group of warriors that were a quarter mile away and thought to himself. *Here we are, fourteen men facing about eighty Comanche probably led by the biggest white hater of them all, Quanah Parker.* He stared out the window for a few seconds. He turned back to his scout. "What do you think?"

"I think we are in a passel of trouble Sir. As far as I know, no other patrol is close by and we are about forty miles from Fort Clark as the crow flies and seventy or eighty by the road. I think the only chance we have Sir is for someone to try to slip out tonight and cut across country to the Fort for help."

"Sergeant Arnold, I know you have been in many engagements with the Apache. What do you think?"

"I have heard the reports like the scout has. There is a good possibility that the warrior could be the war chief of the Quahada's. If so, we'll have our hands full come daylight."

The sun was dropping over the western hills and Booker was at least hoping what he had heard that Indians don't fight at night for one of their beliefs was that if you were killed at night, you would not enter the "spirit world" and wander in darkness forever. Thinking this, he turned back to Bowlegs. "Start a small fire and let the men have some hot coffee and bacon with their biscuits."

"Yes Sir. That be a fine idea Sir. Nothing like hot coffee to boost a man's spirit."

An hour later it was full dark, and the moon had not come up yet as Bowlegs walked his pony east, away from the homestead. He walked several hundred yards leading his horse who had shirts from some of the men wrapped around his hooves to keep the noise down. It worked and he mounted his horse after walking due east for over a very nervous quarter mile. He headed for Clark cross country. Being the horseman, he was he knew he could pace his horse to where he could make it to the fort. It was slow at first but when the moon came up he was able to see and rode at a mile eating gallop and then walked, then galloped.

About one hour after the scout left the Comanche led by Little Bear rode past the troopers screaming and releasing arrows at the men behind the walls. This was before the moon came up and far as the soldiers knew in the dark, from the noise and number of horses figured all the Comanche had left. One man was killed, and another had an arrow in his shoulder. They found two Comanche on the ground that their blind firing had knocked off the ponies. One was dead and the other wounded. The wounded brave cut a trooper's arm as the trooper stupidly rolled him over to see if he was dead like the other. Three other troopers shot the Comanche immediately.

"Arnold, what the hell just happened?

"Beats me, Sir, but looks like for some reason known only to them, they left."

"Why would they do that?"

"Indians are notional and unpredictable Sir. Onliest person I know that has ever seemed to figure them out is Watkins."

"Well, we sure as hell not going to go wandering in the dark and fall into a trap," Booker said. "We'll stay right here behind these walls till daylight. Sergeant, set the night guard shift, at least two watching with one of them watching the horses, then see to the wounded. Arnold saluted and left thinking to himself, *this here wet behind the ears officer just might make it out here if we make it out of this mess. Seems levelheaded and never showed any fear earlier.*

Quanah led twenty warriors south away from their camp as the others stormed by the homestead headed north. Quanah and his men were on foot staying away from the road and being careful not to leave any sign of their passing. It was only about three miles to where he planned his trap. The plan was for Little Bear to go on the other side of the Pecos canyon and wait, watching what the bluecoats did. If they left at daylight, he was to stay a safe distance behind the troopers and be ready to close in when he strung the trap."

~~

It was four in the morning when a tired Bowlegs on an exhausted horse crossed the bridge over Los Moras Creek and into Fort Clark. "Get Major Thurston," he shouted to the guard on duty, "And I don't mean tomorrow." He headed to headquarters and collapsed on the porch. Thurston arrived five minutes later.

"What's happening Mr. Bowlegs?" The scout quickly explained the situation. Thurston turned to the sentry. "Get me Tye Watkins, NOW," he shouted. The sentry almost stumbled over himself leaving. "HOLD ON Private," he shouted. 'On your way stop at Sergeant O'Malley's and tell him to get his ass here and also Lieutenant Harrison and I want a thirty-man patrol ready in thirty minutes with three days rations and thirty rounds of ammunition for their rifles. Ten minutes later there were men scurrying in every direction: troopers getting their gear together, stablemen getting horses saddled, and the ordnance sergeant getting the ammunition ready for the men to pick up.

Tye arrived at headquarters and immediately found Thurston. "What's the emergency Major?" Major Thurston laid out the problem quickly. "I know the homestead you are talking about. You remember Yancey Cates?"

Thurston nodded. "How in the world could anyone forget that murdering scoundrel?"

"Well, the homestead is where that piece of horse manure murdered a whole family: grandfather, parents and three young people. They raped the teenage daughter and the mother in front of the men before killing them all." At that time O'Malley showed up with the patrol and Tye's horse, Sandy. Tye mounted Sandy and reached down to shake

Thurston's hand. "We can cut across country and be there a couple hours after daylight."

"Get going and good luck, "Major Thurston said turning to the troops lined up in front of the headquarters and saluted the men. Tye jumped in the saddle and with Lt. Harrison, led the men across the bridge and turned west on the Old Mail Road. They rode at an easy gallop for a couple miles then turned off the road and cut across country.

Chapter Two

During a brief stop to let the horses blow Tye looked around and realized he recognized only three or four of the men and did not know Lt. Harrison at all. One of the men he knew by only his last name, Private Bailey, walked over to him and stuck out his hand. Tye took it and the man said how glad he was back scouting and not chasing outlaws.

Tye smiled and said, "I'm glad to be back Bailey. Didn't know how much I missed getting up in the middle of the night, eating cold biscuits and hardtack, and riding with a bunch of smelly troopers and chasing Indians." He laughed along with everyone else that was listening.

Before the talk turned to him with a bunch of questions from the troops he walked over to Sandy, but he could hear the men questioning Bailey.

"Damn men," Bailey said holding up his hand. "They will be time for the questions later. Right now, we have friends to try and pull out of a trap. All I'll say for now is, what you have heard about that man is all true and probably under stated." He nodded his head toward a couple of men. "Janson and Morley over there and myself have been on more than one patrol with him and all three of us would be dead, scalped, and buried now if not for him. First Sergeant O'Malley knows him better anyone with maybe the exception of Major Thurston.

The eastern sky was just starting to turn gray when the men at the homestead started moving around. Fuller stirred the coals in the fire from last night and placing small sticks on them had a fire going and coffee on in two pots. Booker and the men still could not figure why all the Comanche left last night, or if all had. They sat around the fire making small talk and drinking coffee until the sun was up.

Lieutenant Booker stood up. "Fuller, you take two men, get your horses and go where the Comanche camp was and scout the area to see if all are gone."

"Yes Sir." He pointed at two men. "Come with me and went behind the homestead and was back a minute later mounted.

"We will have our rifles ready to cover you. If see anything or anyone, don't engage, just get back here. Understood?"

Fuller nodded, saluted and he and the men headed to the camp. As they warily approached the camp, they saw nothing. Arriving, no sign of anyone and the fires were cold. They rode back to the homestead and reported what they saw. Booker wished like hell Bowlegs was here to give him some advice.

"If I may Lieutenant," Sergeant Arnold said. "May I suggest before we leave take the horses down to the Pecos and let them have some water and if I may also suggest something else. This here whole thing with the Comanche leaving like that smells like horse shit. They are up to something and if that was Quanah, he's smarter than hell Sir.

All I'm saying Sir, we need to wait just a little longer and be damn watchful when we leave."

"Noted Sergeant, and we will do just that. I don't like the feel of things either, but I have no experience with the Indians."

"I have had more than I like, and this just smells to high heaven."

"We'll wait an hour," Booker said.

~~

Tye and the men were watering their tired mounts at a spring. Harrison, looking at Tye and watching him move around talking to the men thought to himself. *The man is huge, but he moves like a big cat. Thurston said to believe every damn story you have heard about him because he can vouch for every one of them. Thurston also said he has more scars than all of the men on the fort put together from arrows, bullets, and knives. Hope I have time to sit and talk to him sometime.*

~~

Back at the homestead, Booker figured they had waited long enough so he had Sergeant Arnold muster the men from behind the walls and to their horses. They led their mounts down the road into the canyon to water their horses on the Pecos River, and then mounting them, rode out and past the homestead where every man looked at it knowing the old place had saved their lives.

"Private Fuller," Lieutenant Booker shouted.

Fuller rode up beside the Lieutenant. "Yes Sir."

"Take a man and ride ahead and make sure we are not riding into a trap just in case all the Comanche did not leave last night."

Fuller chose a man and a few seconds later were headed past the column. Three miles down the road just before the road dropped into a small canyon, Arnold had a feeling things were wrong. *If I only learned one thing From Tye over the years, it was to trust a man's gut feelings. They were not right all the time but were enough times right to pay attention, Tye would say,* he thought to himself. He was glad when Booker halted the column before entering the canyon to wait on his scouts.

"I don't like this Lieutenant," he said. "Got me one of those feelings that there is a problem ahead somewhere."

"That's why we are waiting on Fuller to come back and report, Sergeant."

"Yes Sir, I know that but Fuller has not had that much experience out here and may overlook something."

"We won't go any farther till he rides out of that canyon," Booker replied.

~~

Tye and the column arrived at the homestead and was surprised to find no one there. He turned to Lieutenant Harrison. "I think it would be a good idea to have the men water the horses while I scout around see what's going on. He dismounted and taking his rifle from the scabbard, handed his reins to a private and asked him to take care of Sandy for a few minutes.

Harrison turned to Sergeant O'Malley, "Sergeant, have the men take their mounts down to the Pecos and water them." A private rode up and took the Lieutenants reins.

Harrison dismounted and followed Tye wanting to listen to him and maybe learn something.

They walked south on the road and came to where the Comanche camp was. Tye circled the camp saying nothing, much to Harrison's disappointment. Finally, Tye squatted down and Harrison squatted beside him. Nothing was said for a moment the Tye Spoke.

"We have a serious problem Sir. See these unshod pony tracks headed back to and past the homestead. I saw then when we reached to homestead headed down into the canyon and away from the troops holed up there. Now I know why."

Harrison looked at him. "What do you mean?"

See these tracks of the unshod ponies headed north and the see the shod tracks headed south."

"I see that."

"Well, the tracks heading south were after the Comanche tracks heading north which means that the patrol headed south after the Comanche went north. The tracks headed north were made last night and the patrols tracks going south are a little over an hour old. Now, look at the unshod tracks going south. There were made a few minutes ago."

"Are you saying the Comanche are behind the patrol now?"

"Yes Sir, but that's not the only problem." Tye stood up. "Look over here," and he squatted down again and pointed to the sand beside the road. "What do you see?"

"Footprints."

"Yes Sir. Moccasin footprints and a lot of them. I would say twenty to twenty-five sets, all off the road so they would be hard to see."

"Are you saying what I think you are?"

"A lot of the Comanche left last night after dark fooling the Troops into thinking they all left. The rest are down the road apiece waiting to ambush them and the ones that left last night are now following the patrol and when the ambush is sprung, they will close in from behind. A well-planned trap."

"My God!" Harrison exclaimed jumping to his feet. "We have to get mounted and help them out." They trotted back to where the men were waiting with the horses, mounted up, and headed south at an easy gallop. Harrison was still trying to figure how Tye could read all that, but hoped he was wrong. Fifteen minutes they heard gunfire ahead of them and he knew Tye was right.

Earlier, Private Fuller reported back and said they had seen no sign of Indians. Sergeant Arnold mumbled something.

"Did you say something Sergeant?"

"Just thinking out loud Sir."

"Well, out with-it man."

"It's been my experience that when you don't see an Indian that's when you better look out. You will learn Sir that out here the only time you see an Indian is when he wants you to. That canyon right there ahead of us has the hair on the back of my neck standing up even though Fuller saw nothing. I think we had better be ready for trouble and have our side arms out because if there is trouble it will be close in fighting."

Booker didn't think there was any problem, but he valued the Sergeant's opinion so more or less to humor him he told him to have the men pull their side arms and be ready for trouble. They started down the slope into the canyon trotting their mounts with no trouble. When Booker and Arnold at the head of the patrol hit level ground, all hell broke loose.

Chapter Three

Comanche suddenly appeared from everywhere filling the air with war screams and arrows. Booker's mount went down with arrows in him throwing the Lieutenant to the hard road stunning him. Four of the men in the patrol were hit multiple times and were dead before they hit the ground. Fuller had an arrow high in his back and was slumped over his saddle. Others were hit in the legs or shoulders, but one had an arrow in his belly. All of them were managing to stay in the saddle and three or four were firing their Colts.

Arnold turned his mount and as Booker stood up Arnold shouted, "Your hand Sir," And as Booker raised his hand Arnold took hold and swung him onto the saddle behind him like the men all trained for hours doing for situations like this. An arrow hit Arnold in the left shoulder, but he managed to stay in the saddle with Bookers arms around his waist. Seeing several warriors ahead, he led what remained of the patrol into the rocks to the right and holding the reins in his teeth, his left arm hanging useless he shot the only two warriors he saw in the rocks. "

"Dismount," he shouted, "Grab your canteens and Spenser's and find a rock. He looked around as things died down for a minute. He saw the dead troopers on the road and cursed under his breath. He looked at the men left and saw two with an arrow in their leg and one with in his shoulder. He saw one with one in his stomach and then he saw Fuller slumped against a boulder with an arrow in his back. Booker regained his faculties and saw the trouble they were in. He had eight men left and five of them were injured including Arnold.

"What do you think Sergeant?"

"Start praying and get ready to meet your maker, Sir." He heard horses and looked at the top of the canyon. "Shit!" he cursed out loud. "Look there, Sir." Forty or more Comanche were coming over the crest of the hill and heading their way.

As they watched the Comanche stopped about two hundred yards back up the road the troopers had come down. All could tell the newcomers were getting worked up and getting ready to charge and overrun the patrol, what was left of it any way.

Lieutenant hollered at the men. "Get ready and fire at will when they are close enough." Then he added. "Save one bullet for yourself. Do not get taken prisoner." Gloom settled over the little group as all knew there was no hope.

The Comanche, now with their leader who had come out of the rocks and straddled his black pony who were getting more and more worked up as the warrior on the black pony rode back and forth in front of them waving his bow above his head. The men waited, knowing they had only minutes to live.

Suddenly, the screaming stopped, and all of the Comanche turned as one to look back up the road they had just come down. Arnold heard it first.

"A bugle Sir. I think I heard a bugle blowing Sir." A couple seconds later Booker heard it as did the men. Hopes rose. Then, the Comanche turned and charged down the road at them. The soldiers were forty or so yards off the road and the Comanche released their arrows as they charged by them but did not turn to overrun them. The men hunkered down in the rocks were showered with arrows but only three hit flesh, the rest bouncing off the rocks. They now heard the rattling of sabers, and the sound of shod horses rush by them and up the slope before they stopped, turned around and trotted back to the trapped men. The men were standing, those that could, were waving their arms. Booker looked around and saw one man dead and two more wounded. He and one other were the only ones unscathed.

"I be damned," Arnold said. "Sir, that's Tye leading them back down the road."

Tye, Harrison and the troops all dismounted and rushed over to the beleaguered patrol. Lieutenant Harrison was appalled at what he saw. This also was his first encounter with Indians. Tye went to work on the wounded. Both lieutenants were with him and when Tye looked at the soldier with the arrow in his stomach, who was now unconscious, he looked at Harrison and shook his head.

"Sergeant O'Malley," Tye shouted. "Get someone to start a fire and find some shirts from these soldier's saddle bags we can use for wrapping the wounds. He turned to Harrison. "Sir, I need a couple of men to assist me with the wounded and I think it would a good idea to put a couple of men on the top of both sides of the canyon to make sure the Comanche doesn't come back and surprise us while we are caring for the wounded.

Harrison turned to Sergeant O'Malley to get him to do this but smiled when he saw the Sergeant already selecting the men. *Guess he overheard Tye,* he thought to himself. While Tye was looking after the wounded, he and Booker had time to talk for the first time.

"Never been so glad to see anyone in my life as I was when ya'll came over the top of the canyon blowing that bugle", he said smiling and shaking Harrison's hand.

"You can thank the scout Bowlegs and then thank that man over there," he said nodding his head toward Tye. "I learned today a lot about him and why the men think so much of him. Let me ask you something. Did most of the Comanche leave last night and did you leave this morning not knowing all did not leave?

Booker nodded. "Yes."

Tye read sign this morning at the homestead and told me exactly that. He also found the tracks of the ones that went to this canyon on foot and told me they would be waiting for you there. And then he told me the bunch that left last had doubled back and were going to be here shortly after the ambush was sprung."

"He could tell all that by studying the tracks?" Booker asked astonishment showing in his voice.

"Yep! Not only read where the tracks were going but knew just about the time they were made."

Harrison removed is hat and took is kerchief from around his neck and wiped his face with it. "I think Lieutenant, that we have a lot to learn out here," he chuckled.

They both watched as Tye moved from one wounded trooper to another and showing how arrows were removed and cauterized with a hot knife blade. The soldier who had been hit in the belly had died and he along with the ones cut down in the ambush had been wrapped in blankets and tied across a saddle for the ride back to Fort Clark. When the last wounded man had been taken care of Tye approached the two lieutenants along with First Sergeant O'Malley and Sergeant Arnold.

"I think the wounded can be helped on their horses and head back to the fort when you two are ready."

"I haven't mentioned this Tye," Arnold said, "but me and Bowlegs think that bunch of Comanche were led by Quanah Parker."

Tye, who had been sitting on a large boulder jumped to his feet. "What makes you think that?" "Well, the reports we had was that he was rather large for a Comanche, always wore and single eagle feather in his hair and rode a black horse. The warrior leading them fit the description." Arnold answered.

Tye turned back to the lieutenants. "May I make a suggestion?" Both men nodded their heads. "We need to know if that was Quanah because if it was, our troubles are just beginning. He has forty or fifty braves with him, more than enough to raise bloody hell around here. I would like one of you to pick fifteen men and go with me to track them and find out. If it is not him, we still have a problem with that many warriors, but if it is Quanah, we have a lot more trouble to deal with. The others can take the dead and wounded along with the other fifteen men we came out with and go to the Fort. I know both of you are new and do not know the area yet so First Sergeant O'Malley can go with you to the fort. I would like Sergeant Arnold, if he is able to ride, to go with me." He looked at the two men.

"Ain't no damn arrow in the shoulder going to keep me from chasing that heathen," Arnold said.

"I think you are right, Tye," Harrison said. "I know you," nodding toward Booker, "have got to be exhausted so I think it reasonable I go with Tye and you go back to the fort and report to Thurston," With that said he turned to Sergeant Arnold. "Sergeant, pick fifteen men to go with Tye and myself.

"Yes Sir," Arnold said saluting and walking away to pick the men. Ten minutes later, the men were ready to go to the fort and the others were riding away with Tye. Tye, in a quick look at the men Arnold had picked, saw they were not all young green troops. He saw the three men he knew from previous patrols he had seen earlier, Bailey, Jason and Morley.

With Tye in front and Harrison and Arnold with the other men left following the tracks of the Comanche. Thirty minutes later Tye reined in Sandy, dismounted to study the tracks. A few seconds later the patrol arrived.

"What's the matter Tye," Lieutenant Harrison asked.

"The Comanche split into three groups of about fifteen or twenty each. One is going on straight ahead and the other two in different directions, one south and one north."

"Why do you figure they did that?"

"Two possibilities Sir: One, they probably know we are following them and hope we split our troops up and follow the three set of tracks, or two, they are setting up another ambush. I'm figuring on the latter."

"So, what do you think we should do?"

"Let's you, Arnold, and me talk about it for a few minutes while the men take a break and check their weapons."

"Weapons?"

"I've got a feeling they are going to need them pretty damn quick Lieutenant and nothing worse can happen to a man when he needs them if they are dirty and not working right or thought they were fully loaded and they were not. When you are leading a patrol Lieutenant, it's always best to plan for the worse and give yourself a chance to survive if it comes. If it doesn't, then be happy it didn't and live to see another day. Remember this Sir, the Apache, the Comanche, and the other tribes did not go to West Point and study the rules of war fare, they make their own rules, and they are damn good at it. Even if you know the book on rules of war word for word, they don't make a tinker's damn out here. Sergeant Arnold and I have seen plenty of Lieutenants come out here fresh from The Point and get themselves and men under them killed by trying to go by the book." Trust your gut feelings about things, listen to men like Arnold here who have been around for a while, and you might just make it."

Tye chuckled, "Enough of my preaching let's cut to the problem. "

Harrison said, "I think you are going to follow the tracks going east or at least I think I would. Can you keep us from an ambush?"

Arnold laughed at that last part of what the Lieutenant said. "Sir, Tye has led God only knows how many patrols and only one was ambushed and that was because a Captain would not listen to him."

"Well, there's always a first time Sergeant," Tye said smiling. "To answer your question Lieutenant, yes, I think I can."

"Let's get on with it then."

As they traveled following the tracks. Harrison was studying the barren landscape and like others before him, wondered why in hell all the settlers were coming out here.

No trees, rocky ground and lots of cactus and obviously not a lot of rain were his observations of the land.

Sergeant Arnold noticed the lieutenant studying the land and smiled. "You wondering why in hell all these people are coming out here Lieutenant?"

Surprised by the question he replied. "Well, yes I was as a matter of fact."

"Don't you feel like you are alone in that feeling? Truth is, just about everyone that comes here, I'm talking about officers and enlisted men, feel the same way...at first. But this land grows on you, and you will come to appreciate it for what it is. It looks the same today as it did a hundred years ago and will look the same in another 100 years. You will learn to respect the men and women who come here to make a life for themselves and their children. You might even to learn to respect the Apache and Comanche."

"Respect the savages?"

"Don't let Tye hear you say that."

"Say what, respect the savages?"

"I'm going to give you a little speech that I have heard Tye give many times to the troops when on patrol when he hears the word, savages, by some of the men. First of all, scalping of the enemy did not start with the Apache, it started when the Mexican government who put a bounty on Apache scalps a few years ago and it did not matter if it was a man's, woman's, or child's. When Tye was young, his only friend was an Apache boy, and he spent a lot of time in Apache camps. The word lie is not in the Apache tongue. We have to lock our doors at night or when we are gone from our home. An Apache can leave his belongings in his wickiup or outside it and things will be as he left it when he returns. They are a loving people who worship their children. They have been in this land for generations, and they are simply fighting to keep it, to live the way their fathers and grandfathers lived…free. That's it in a nutshell Lieutenant. Tye's speech would be much longer. Tye does not hate the Indian, he respects them. I can tell you how much they respect Tye as a warrior. They have put out what we would call a wanted poster on him and the warrior who kills him will be greatly honored by this tribe. Do you know how long he has been fighting Apaches?" The lieutenant shook his head. "He killed his first with a knife when he was fourteen and…" he stopped because Tye was riding back to them.

Tye reined Sandy in and threw his right leg over the pommel of his saddle. It's going to be dark in an hour or so Sir. I found a good place to camp ahead and if I may suggest we camp early and give everyone a chance to get some rest. Last twelve or so hours have been tough on the men and the horses."

"Are we close to the Comanche?"

"Close enough to be damn careful."

"You are right about the men needing rest. Truth is, my butt could use a little rest from the saddle," he chuckled. "Sergeant Arnold, see that the men know we are making camp shortly." Twenty minutes later they were at where Tye wanted to camp, and Arnold chuckled loud enough for Tye and Harrison to hear.

"What's so funny Sergeant?" Harrison asked.

"I was just looking at this camp site, Sir. I have been on so many patrols with Tye and know what he looks far as a camp site. I could have picked this place just from I know he looks far."

"And what that might be."

"Look around Sir. There is a clear area on two sides which makes it pretty easy to defend and on west side there is so much cactus and brush it is impossible to get through even on foot without making a lot of noise besides getting a lot of cactus needles in you. Behind the camp is a steep slope that is steep enough horses will have a serious problem climbing and a Indian would spend more time just trying to get up to us than they would shooting arrows."

Harrison looked around and nodded his head in agreement with what the Sergeant said. Tye spoke up.

"That's one thing you need to learn when you are leading a patrol and that is to learn the lay of the land and remember the location of the springs and camping sites. When selecting a camp site, find a defendable place even if there has been no trouble for a while. Remember Lieutenant, one mistake our here just might get yourself and your men killed. This land out here can kill you too. Water can get scarce at times and that's why you need to know where the springs are that are reliable to always have water and there is not many of them. In fact, I bet you the Comanche are camped about five miles from us at a spring that I know always has water."

"If we are that close, why didn't we go ahead and attack the camp."

"Because if that is Quanah, he will expect that and probably the other two parties are converging on that spot, and we will be fighting fifty or so instead of fifteen. Don't underestimate the Indians. They have been fighting for as long as one can remember. An Apache boy is a warrior and probably has killed his first enemy by the time he is fifteen or sixteen years old. Their childhood is not exactly like ours. When they can walk, they are put on horses and learn to ride. At five or six instead of playing games we played, they are playing war games. They become proficient at using a knife, tomahawk, and bow at an early age. Do not fall into believing they are at a real disadvantage because they don't have many rifles. Most of the time battles are close in and at around sixty yards the Apache or Comanche is as accurate with a bow as you are with a gun."

"What is the plan?"

"I'm gonna find their camp after dark and see what I can learn. If it is Quanah then I am going to talk to him."

"You are going talk to him? Are you crazy?"

Tye looked around and saw that the Lieutenants outburst was loud enough it go the men's attention. He smiled and answered the lieutenant. "Crazy maybe, but Quanah and I met once, and I think he will remember me and will talk. He speaks pretty good English, and I would like to know why they are this this far south.

"And if he don't want to talk?"

"I guess you will be short a scout," he chuckled. No one laughed. "Actually, most Indian tribes will not kill an unarmed man that comes into their camp of his own free will. They respect that. I would like a volunteer to go with me." He looked to where the man was gathered and saw no hands then a man stood up…Private Bailey.

"I'll go with you Tye."

Tye was glad it was Bailey. He knew him to be tough and handled himself well in a fight. Bailey walked to where Tye and the Lieutenant were. Tye stuck out his hand and shook Bailey's. Bailey turned to the Lieutenant. "Private Richard Bailey, Sir." Harrison returned the salute of the private and then shook his hand.

"What's your first name Private Bailey?"

"Harold Dickie Bailey, Sir. Onliest name I answer to is Dick or Dickie."

"Dickie Bailey it is then. What's the plan Tye?"

"We will find the camp and watch to see if I see Quanah. If we do, Dickie here will keep watch and make sure the horses are kept quiet. That's it in a nutshell Sir."

"When do you leave?"

"Soon as its starts getting dark." He turned to Bailey. Go back to your fire and eat something and drink some coffee. Make sure you have a full canteen in case we are stuck out there for a while." When Bailey turned to leave Tye said, "Glad it was you Dickie." Dickie walked back to his fire standing a little taller and proud of himself. He would change his mind later.

When the sun had dropped behind the low hills in the west, Tye and Bailey left the camp. They traveled for several minutes with nothing being said which made Bailey a little more nervous, after all they were possibly walking into a Comanche camp with possibly the biggest white man hater of all. No problem he told himself and shuddered. Finally Tye spoke.

"We'll dismount over there Dickie. Dickie wondered at first why Tye decided here, then he heard it: faint sounds of men talking. "The camp is just over the hill. There is a spring there with good cold water. I figured if they come across it they would camp. We need to sneak as close as we can and be damn quiet. Take your sword off and your spurs. Take the crossed sword emblem off your hat. We don't want anything that might reflect the light from the fires."

These things done, Tye put his hand on the private's shoulder and quietly said, "Move slow, stay behind me and watch where you step. A twig snapping can be heard a long ways." They moved silently thru the brush toward the fires. Tye was looking for guards, but he did not see any and they were only forty yards from the camp. Bailey figured the damned Comanche could probably hear his heart beating. It felt like it was coming out of his chest. He could not spit his mouth was so dry and looking at his hands they were shaking. Tye tapped him on the shoulder and nodded to the middle of the camp. "That's him. That's Quanah," he whispered.

Dickie was afraid he could not even walk but knew he had been in several fights with the Apache and felt like this and handled himself very well.

Tye whispered, "Go back to the horses and wait for me. I'm going down to the camp."

"You sure you don't want me to go with you?" He whispered back. Tye shook his head.

"Go back toward the horses but don't lose sight of the camp and watch..." He stopped talking more warriors rode into the camp from the north. All the Comanche were excited and shouting. "That eliminates my idea of going in Dickey. No way would I get a chance to talk to Quanah now. Let's head back to the camp.

Arriving at the camp he reported what had happened. "Quanah is leading them. I was going into the camp to talk when more came in from the north"

"Do you think it was the ones that split off the trail we were following?"

"It's possible but I don't think so. If the ones that broke off to the south would had to go back north and we would have seen their tracks as they crossed the tracks we were following. I think it was a new bunch that was already coming down and Quanah sent a runner to bring him to this spring where they were going to camp."

"Good God!" Harrison exclaimed. "That means there are one hundred or more."

"Don't get excited Lieutenant, Tye whispered, "the men are watching. I have a plan and it's going to sound crazy to you but I think it will work." He turned to Arnold. How's the shoulder Sergeant?"

"Hurts like hell but I'm able to ride and fight."

"Good. Do you remember the canyon where we first fought Tanza two years ago?" Arnold nodded. We are no more than twenty miles north of Fort Clark. If you can ride to the fort and tell Thurston the situation here and have a full troop of Calvary meet us there tomorrow as early as possible. Can you do that?"

"Sure nu'ff Tye."

"This is my plan Lieutenant and tell me what you think." Tye paused for a second. I'll get around the camp and find their horse herd. I can take Bailey with me. I'll leave Bailey hidden close to the herd and then I will come back here. We can get the troops a decent night's sleep and then move them close to the Comanche camp before first light. When I fire my colt it will be a signal for Bailey to shoot the one or two guards at the pony herd and then stampede them. We will make one run through the camp and on to the east. We should be able to kill several of them and mess up whatever plans they have because they will spend a lot of time rounding up their horses. We can then meet Bailey and the troop at the place we discussed. This will really piss them off and their knowing how few we will be coming for the kill with blood in their eyes as soon as they gather their horses. They will not expect a full troop of soldiers waiting for them."

"I can see that Tye, but do you think it's a good idea to have fifteen men attack a force of possibly one hundred Comanche?"

"Probably not but look at it this way Sir. There are settlers all over this country and we have patrols out. What chance do the settlers have or what chance one of our patrols have if they stumble onto one hundred Comanche accidently not knowing they were around. We can hit the camp just as they are waking up and be through them before they know what is happening. Even if we don't kill any of them by stampeding their horse herd they will be crippled for a while. When they do round of their horses they will come after us with blood in their eyes and hopefully we can trap them if the troop from Clark shows up on time."

Harrison was silent for a moment then said, "Sounds like a good plan but what happens if the troops don't show up?"

"Pray," Tye chuckled. "I do think it would be a good idea for you to talk to the men and tell them the plan." They both walked to where the men were as Arnold rode out headed toward the fort. When the men were gathered Lieutenant Harrison spoke.

"I know some of you, like myself, have not been in a fight with Indians before. This situation here is why you are in the Calvary. Our obligation is to keep this country safe for those good people trying to make a living out here. In the morning we are going to attack the Comanche camp. We are going to hit hard and fast and should be through the camp in a few seconds. In those seconds we can kill a few of them and disrupt their plans. Bailey here will be in position to stampede their horse herd. We will then go to a place and wait for Arnold to get there with a full troop from Clark. When we go in use your Colts, lay low over the saddle and fire at anything that moves. Any questions?"

One trooper spoke up. "Aren't there a hundred or so Comanche, Sir?"

Tye said, "You are right trooper. About eight or so of them to one of us. I'd say the odds are in our favor, wouldn't you." There was a round of nervous laughter in the troops.

Another soldier spoke up. "Tye, we all know of your exploits fighting Apaches and outlaws. I think I speak for all of us when I say you can damn sure count on us to follow the Lieutenant and you into hell if need be." There were a lot of and nodding of heads and men saying they were ready. Being a soldier at a fort with no combat experience can be troubling for a man who was sorter looked down on by the veteran troops. This was their chance to be one of the men at the fort who had fought the Indians and would be accepted with a little more respect.

"Good. Get some rest and I will see you in the morning…early," Tye said laughing. "Private Bailey can you come with the Lieutenant and me?" A moment later the three of them squatted by the Lieutenants and Tye's bedrolls. "You heard the Lieutenants plan for in the morning?"

"Yes Sir."

Tye chuckled, "You just volunteered for another assignment."

Bailey laughed. "I'm getting real good at volunteering. What did I volunteer for this time?"

"We, you and me, are going back to the Comanche camp in a little while. We are going to find the horse herd and you are going to keep watch until dawn is breaking. When you hear the first gun shot from us charging the camp you will kill the one or two sentries and stampede their horses. You need to pick a man to go with us so one of you can stand watch while the others gets some sleep."

"Yes Sir. I will get Private Morley, if that's okay with the Lieutenant." Harrison nodded. He walked over to where Morley lay on his blanket and nudged him with his boot. "Don't go going to sleep Morley. You just volunteered for a special assignment."

Morley raised up and put his hat on. "Whut the hell did I vonteer fer?"

"A good chance to get killed."

"Great! Whut do I do and when do I do it?"

55

"Get some rest and I'll come get you."

"Wrest! How in hell do you think I can wrest when I'm gonna die?"

Bailey walked to his blanket smiling and thinking, *I love that old boy like a brother and love the ways he talks. He's and old mountain boy from Tennessee and I know he can knock the eye out of a rabbit at fifty yards and ain't afraid of the devil himself. It will be a comfort to me not to be by myself and with someone I can count on.* With that thought he dosed off.

A couple hours later, Tye nudged both of them awake and the three of them walked back to where the Lieutenant was. Tye looked at the two privates. "Let's go."

Chapter Four

While the three men rode toward the Comanche camp Tye explained exactly what they were to do. "There will be one maybe two at most watching the herd. I will locate the herd while the two of you wait with the horses. When I locate them I will come back and get you and take you there where you will hide and wait till daybreak. When we charge the camp, kill the ones watching the herd by any means you can, then stampede the horses away from camp. When we get through the camp we will have your horses and we will get the hell on down the road to where hopefully Arnold has a full troop waiting for us.

When they were three or so hundred yards from the camp Tye halted Sandy and the three dismounted. He looked at Morley. "Go ahead and take off your cross-swords emblem on your hat and your spurs and anything that might reflect light or rattle. I'll be back shortly.

A few minutes later he was watching the camp and saw Quanah talking with two other warriors. The two with Quanah were excited about something and were talking loud enough for Tye to hear. *Wish I could understand their lingo*, Tye thought to himself. *They are sure excited about something.*

Quanah listened to the two men tell him about the soldiers from Fort Davis they had killed and three homes they had burned and the men, women, and children they had killed. They wanted more of the same. He stood up. "I too want to kill all the white people who are coming into this land. But first, I want to kill the bluecoats that killed our brothers. They will be following us and we will trap them tomorrow. You have ridden far and fought well, now get some rest."

Tye worked his way around the camp to the east side and as he thought, there was the horse herd. Moving silently thru the brush he began searching for the guards. The moon had not come up yet and it was dark as sin. He heard a twig break just in front of him. He waited, being still and barely breathing. He drew his knife from its sheath in his right knee-high moccasin and waited. A minute, then two went by then suddenly a warrior stood up not four feet in front of him and spoke to another brave. The other answered back and Tye got a general idea where he was by his voice. No other words were spoken.

Tye started to backtrack when he heard at least two more talking to his left. *They are replacing these men*, he thought. He hunkered lower so he was beneath the tops of the brush and waited. He listened to the two new braves talking to the ones that had been guarding the herd. After a minute, the two who had been watching left to go back to the camp. The two new guards stood four or five feet away and were talking. Tye waited a few more minutes until the men walked away to settle down and watch the herd before moving back around the camp the way he had come and to Bailey and Morley.

"Damn Tye," Bailey said. "We thought you had run into trouble or something."

"No trouble but they just changed guards while I was there watching the horse herd. If you have ever moved quietly before, now is the time to do it again, only quieter. Follow me and like I said be quiet. Watch where you step so you don't kick a rock or break a twig. Slowly they made their way around the camp till Tye held his hand up to stop. He had the men lean in close to him.

Tye spoke in a soft whisper. Ya'll stay here behind this brush. When we hit the camp the guards will likely stand up to see what is going on. Kill them if you can but just make sure you stampede the horses by any means necessary. Understood?" Both men nodded. "Okay, settle your butts down, get comfortable. One of you keep watch at all times and be ready at first light.

An hour later Tye rode back into the camp and immediately got his tin cup from his saddle bag and strolled over the small fire and lifting the coffee pot poured a cup of coffee. He was surprised when Lieutenant Harrison walked over to him and poured himself a cup and squatted by the fire.

"How did it go Tye?"

Tye explained to him that the men were set and knew what to do. There is a small hill just this side of the camp, the top no more than two hundred yards from the camp. If we are quiet we can get men almost to the crest and attack from there. It's all downhill then and we should hit the camp fifteen or so seconds later. The Comanche will be surprised but if they are like the Apache they will put up a defense very quickly."

"Do you think we all will make it through the camp?"

"Yes, if a horse is not shot. I will have the men tie themselves to the saddle to keep from falling off if they are hit with an arrow or if a warrior tries to pull them off. Last thing a man wants is to be taken alive."

"When do we break camp?"

"About an hour before sunup ." Tye looked up at the sky looking at the stars. It's about midnight now so let's get a little sleep while we can."

Harrison went over to his bedroll, sat down and took out his watch. He smiled and shook his head. The watch showed it to be ten minutes after twelve.

Tye woke up an hour before daylight and rousted Lieutenant Harrison. Harrison had a private get the other troopers up. Ten minutes later, horses were saddled, and the men sat in the saddle. Harrison went over the plan again in detail including assigning two men to make sure Bailey's and Morley's horses were with them. All the men rechecked their Colt single action revolvers to make sure they were loaded and in good working order. A few minutes later they were on their way to the Comanche camp, Tye, Harrison, and twelve very nervous soldiers following them.

At the horse herd Bailey was waking up Morley. It was barely becoming gray in the east. Bailey had located the two guards, one was about forty yards away and the other maybe sixty or seventy yards away. Bailey whispered, "You take the one closest and I will take the other. When you hear the first shot from the camp they will undoubtedly stand up to see what's going on and that's when we will shoot. Morley nodded his head. They waited, both a little nervous.

'~~

Arnold had reached the fort about midnight and explained the situation and Tye's plan to Major Thurston. Thurston had an orderly get First Sergeant Jameson and have him pick a thirty-man patrol of battle tested men, no greeners. While the detail was getting together Arnold visited the surgeon to get is shoulder looked at and treated properly.

"The surgeon asked. "Who fixed this up for you Sergeant?"

"Tye did Sir."

"Thought so. Looked like his work. He did a good job," then chuckled, "Lord knows he has had enough practice on himself and others."

Arnold laughed. "Ain't it the truth? Back at the ambush site you would have thought he was an army doctor instead of a scout."

The surgeon nodded his head. "Yes. I cleaned most of them up and didn't have to do a lot to any of them that he hadn't done except put medicine on the wounds. You sure you are up to another ride with that shoulder?"

Arnold nodded. "I figure it's gonna be hurting whether I stay here and lie in bed or ride a horse. Besides, I'm not sure any of the other men know the place Tye is talking about meeting and if we aren't there, Tye and his bunch are in serious trouble."

"Well good luck then. Here, take this with you and if it gets to hurting to bad, take a small swallow. It will make the pain a little less but if you take too much you may fall off your horse because you go to sleep and break your fool neck." Arnold took the bottle and left. The surgeon shook his head and thought, *three meals a day, sometimes that is, hours in the saddle and then a few minutes of sheer terror. These damn soldiers are tougher than nails and for thirteen dollars a month!"* He shook his head again.

Arnold, with a fresh horse, made his way back to headquarters where he found the troops lined up in front with Thurston on the porch. Arnold, his arm in a sling rode up in front of the major and saluted.

"You okay Sergeant?"

"Yes Sir. Ready to go Sir."

"Very well then. First Sergeant Jameson, you will lead the men but listen to First Sergeant Arnold. Understood?"

Jameson saluted, Yes Sir, understood Sir." He and Arnold rode to the front of the horses.

"By the twos HO!" Jameson shouted. The line quickly formed two abreast and rode out of the fort. Arnold, riding beside Jameson filled the lieutenant in on where they were going and what was going to happen if things went according to Tye's plan.

"You know Tye very well?"

Arnold nodded. "Know him about as well as anyone I guess. Been on a lot of patrols he scouted for."

"I've only met him once about a week ago when he walked into Thurston's office when I was there. Seems to be a very pleasant man unlike the stories I have heard.

Arnold laughed. "Yes. Sir he can be as pleasant as anyone. The difference is when he has his hackles up and then you hope it ain't you he's pissed at. That man can be meaner than any Apache you ever saw. Been fighting them about his whole life and they are afraid of him and if you know anything about an Apache, they ain't afraid of anything. They hate him because he thinks like they do and fights with knives, tomahawk, or gun better than they do."

"So I've heard. Besides being a great fighter why do the men think so much of him?"

"That's easy to answer. Like I said he thinks like an Apache and not one patrol he has scouted for as been ambushed besides one and that was because the officer would not listen to him. My advice to you if you ever asked, would be to listen to him before you make a decision that could put your men in danger." A few minutes later he said, "We need to leave the road here Sir, and head cross country." They did.

~~

On the hill overlooking the Comanche camp Tye and Harrison had the men in a skirmish line. When Tye saw the men were ready he nodded to Harrison.

"Give them hell Men! He and Tye jumped their horses into a run down the hill followed by screaming troopers. They hit the edge of the camp and Tye fired at the first Comanche he saw and watched the brave tumble backwards and fall into the coals of a fire. All hell broke loose as the men opened up firing as fast as they could cock their guns and fire. Tye reached the edge of camp and stopping and turning Sandy around. He was picking targets and offering cover fire for the soldiers not yet through the camp. He saw one trooper swaying in the saddle with an arrow in his back as he rushed by. Another trooper came by close to Tye with a Comanche on his back preparing to bash the soldiers head in with a tomahawk when Tye shot the warrior in the head as they rode by. The Comanche was blown sideways off the back of the horse as blood and gore spewed everywhere. Tye took one more look at the camp and glimpsed who he thought was Quanah.

Quanah stood in the camp watching the soldiers leave and saw the man he knew as Watkins. A second later he heard their horses being stampeding and grew even more furious. He shouted to the stunned warriors to catch up with the horses and bring them back. He knew the horses would only run for a mile or so if not driven by the soldiers and he didn't think they would keep driving them. He knew his warriors could round them up and be back in a couple three hours and then he would chase the patrol and wipe them out to the last man. *I hope Watkins is taken alive and we will see how brave he is*," he thought to himself.

All the troopers made it through the camp mainly because they were tied to their saddles. One had an arrow high in his back and one had a nasty cut on his head from a blow by a tomahawk. They stopped to let their mounts blow after about two miles and to see how they were. Tye saw that Bailey and Morley were with them. He walked over and shook both men's hands and congratulated them on a job well done.

After canvasing the men Tye figured they had killed or at least wounded, about ten warriors counting the two he killed. *Not bad*, he thought. *Men shooting from the back of a running horse and in the dark, not bad at all.*

"How long before you figure the Comanche will be on our trail?" Lieutenant Harrison asked.

"Couple hours maybe less. I'm planning on the latter so we probably should get back on the horses and head east to the rendezvous place I told Sergeant Arnold about. "We're about an hour or so out. I'm hoping that Arnold and the men from Clark will be there waiting. I'm going to check on the two men that were wounded before we leave."

Tye walked over where the wounded men were. He saw immediately that the arrow in the troopers back was probably in a lung and the soldier with the head wound only had a headache and was otherwise fine. Looking closer at the man with the arrow in his back he saw bloody froth around his lips, a sure sign of a lung being punctured.

He put his hand on the man's shoulder. "Can you ride for an hour and then we can get that arrow out?" The man nodded which Tye knew he would say yes. He was Calvary and tougher than nails. "Let's move out Lieutenant."

Chapter Five

Little Bear and Broken hand had showed up at the camp with their thirty warriors. Quanah quickly filled them on what happened and that it was Watson leading them.

Little Bear spoke. This Watkins is a little crazy or very brave to attack a Comanche camp with so many warriors and he had so few men."

"Probably a little of both but when we attack them I hope he is taken alive, and we will see just how brave he is." At that time the first of the warriors were returning with the horses. A few minutes later more returned with horses including Quanah's magnificent Black. With the braves that come in with Broken Hand and Little Bear he had more than a hundred blood-thirsty warriors. He leaped onto the blacks back and gathered all around him. By nightfall this day we will be celebrating a great victory over the bluecoats. With much shouting they headed east following the trail of the soldiers.

~~

About nine that morning Tye arrived at the rendezvous place and no Arnold or troops. He pointed out places the soldiers needed to hunker down and be ready for the Comanche. He walked to the man with the arrow in his back. He was barely alive and anyone else would have fallen from his horse. *Tough sonofabitch*, Tye thought to himself. The man passed out as Tye rolled him over on his stomach. *Best thing that could happen*, he thought. Harrison came over to see and Tye shook his head. "The arrow punctured a lung Lieutenant. Not much we can do out here. He needs a surgeon. The best we can do is keep him warm and as comfortable as possible. His passing out is a God send for him."

A few minutes later they all heard it: horses shod hooves striking rocks, rattling sabers, squeaking of the saddles and an occasional cough of one of the troopers. This, the noise made by the Calvary, only proved to Tye why the army could never sneak up on the Indians. Arnold made his way to the Lieutenant and Tye.

"Good to see you made it Sergeant," Tye said shaking Arnold's hand.

"Tye, this Lieutenant Jameson."

Tye took the man's hand. "I think we have met haven't we Lieutenant?"

"Yes Sir, in the major's office a couple weeks ago."

Tye nodded. "We don't have any time to spare Lieutenant. They are going to come at us hard and fast. As you can see, we are a little under maned. I would like to see ten of your soldiers here with us. If you will Sir' take half of your men and place them on the left rim of this canyon and half on the right side. Stay hidden until you hear us firing then have your men come to the edge and open up. We will have them in a crossfire and can do some real damage."

"See to it Sergeant Arnold."

"Yes Sir." Arnold quickly picked ten men to stay in the canyon floor and repeated what Tye said about getting on the rims and stay out of sight."

Jameson and Arnold stayed with Tye and Harrison on the canyon floor and found place for protection from the arrows that would be coming.

Jameson asked. "How long Tye?"

"I'd say about five minutes Lieutenant." Then all the men heard it. A hundred plus ponies running all out makes enough noise to wake the dead. The Comanche came into sight, and they immediately spotted the bluecoats and halted the charge. They milled around a moment then with blood curdling war cries charged the troops. At sixty yards the men in the canyon opened up and several ponies were still coming minus their riders. A wave of arrows came into the boulders where the men were with most glancing off the boulders, but a few found flesh. Almost immediately another wave came in with the same results. One arrow hit Jameson in the upper thigh, and one sliced a gash across Tye's upper left arm. The soldiers on the rims opened up emptying more ponies of their riders. Most of the Comanche realized they had ridden into a trap and halted their charge and rode back a couple hundred yards. Some, not realizing the trap, were now on the soldiers and leaping from the backs of their ponies and smashing into the troops on the canyon floor.

Hand to hand fighting with a wild Comanche-a soldier's worse nightmare. Screams of the wounded and dying filled the canyon. Tye leapt up swinging his Bowie with his right hand and his tomahawk with his left and leaving a devastating path as he moved forward. Jameson and Harrison watched in awe for few seconds before Harrison joined the fight with his sabers. It was over in less than two minutes. Arnold counted seven dead Comanche in Tye's wake. It was suddenly dead silent in the canyon.

"Damn Tye, you must be getting old. I only counted seven you sent to the happy hunting grounds."

An exhausted Tye sat on a boulder, blood dripping off both his Bowie and his tomahawk. "You may be right Arnold." He turned to Harrison. "We better check on the troops Sir."

Harrison, getting over the display of fighting ability of Tye that he just witnessed nodded his head. Tye walked over to Jameson and looked at the arrow in his thigh.

"Congratulations Lieutenant," he said smiling. "You just become a veteran." He knelt down and looked closer at the wound. The arrow went through his thigh and protruded about six inches on the back of his thigh. Tye cut the shaft into below the flint tip. This is going to hurt some, but it has to be done. He rolled the lieutenant onto his side with the injured leg on top. "I'm going to count to three and jerk the shaft out the backside of your leg. You ready?" Jameson nodded. "One, Two and he jerked the shaft out." Tye did note that Jameson did not cry out even though he knew that hurt like hell.

Tye looked up where Harrison stood and looked back up the trail where Harrison was looking. There he was, the "she-bear" of the Comanche, Quanah Parker, sitting on his black with a rag tied to his bow.

"Don't anyone fire their weapon," he shouted. "Come on Lieutenant. This could be interesting." He wiped the blood off his hand with the sand of the canyon floor and started walking towards Quanah.

"Hello Quanah Parker, war chief of the Quahada's."

"Hello to you Tye Watkins," speaking in perfect English much to the amazement of Harrison.

Quanah smiled. "All I have heard of you is true. I just wanted to tell you that I will be back with five times the number of warriors you have seen today. I will kill you and all the stinking bluecoats at what you call Fort Clark. I will take yours and their wives and children and make slaves of them. This I promise." He turned his pony around and rode back to the others.

Walking back to the troops Tye looked up to the rim and signaled the men to come down. In a couple minutes there were on the floor with the horses. "Sergeant Arnold. Get a detail and pick up the dead Comanche and lay them in a row out there and Sergeant, I will shoot any man that does not carry them and lay them down gently." The men believed him.

"Let's see to the dead and wounded of our men, Lieutenant." Two hours later after wrapping the dead in blankets and treating the wounded, they headed back to the fort. They had six dead and eight, counting the Lieutenant, wounded. They had gathered up thirty-five dead warriors and Tye figured they had half again that many licking wounds.

On the way back to Clark Harrison was picking Tye's brain on what he saw during the short battle. "Why is it that the troops had no idea how to fight close in, hand to hand?"

"I intend to speak to Major Thurston about that very thing. Soldiers died today and some unnecessarily. I would be willing to help train them in how to handle a knife."

Lieutenant Harrison chuckled, "From what I seen you do today with a knife and tomahawk I would stand with you when you speak to Thurston."

"I learned at an early age Lieutenant that when you fight close in with a warrior you have to be as mean and vicious as he is or you are going to die. That's why I go sorter go crazy when I am in a hand-to-hand fighting situation. I sometimes scream louder than they do, and it seems to startle them to see a white man doing that."

"When did you kill your first Indian?"

"We were camping, my pa and me that is, and at daybreak we were attacked by three Apaches. Pa killed one right off with his butcher knife and was wrestling the other two. They paid me no mind since I was just a snot nosed kid. I stepped in and stabbed one of them in the back of the neck and then again in the back. Pa killed the other one. To answer your question, I was fourteen at the time. After that incident, Pa, who made quite a name for himself while trapping in the Rockies with Jim Bridger, spent hours teaching me the ins and outs of close in fighting including the dirty tricks one could use and ones to look for from the person you are fighting. He had already had me proficient in tracking and reading sign."

"I'd have to say from what I seen a little while ago he taught you well." Tye nodded to the Lieutenant and rode ahead. Harrison turned in the saddle and spoke to Sergeant Arnold. "Did I say something wrong?"

Arnold laughed and answered the question. "No Sir, you didn't. After you have been around Tye a while you will learn that despite whatever he does that's hard to believe, he does not like to talk about himself. He will ride off or find a reason to check on his horse or some other reason to excuse himself. He's the most modest man I have ever met. Hell Sir, if I was him I would walk around with my chest stuck out and strutting like a rooster saying look at me," he said laughing.

~~

Fifty miles to the north a fifteen-man patrol from Fort Concho (At present day San Angelo) led by Lieutenant Jim Harris patrolled the southern edge of their territory. Unknown to him Quanah and his band of angry Comanche had spotted him while they were headed north to their camp after their encounter with Tye and the Calvary from Fort Clark.

With no trouble having been reported, the men of C troop rode easy in the saddle wishing they were back at Fort

Concho drinking cool beer and not paying a hell of lot attention like they should have. They were daydreaming when their scout came over a nearby hill like the devil was after him. Sliding his horse on his haunches and raising a cloud of dust he told the lieutenant that a hell of lot of Comanche were just over the hill and coming fast. Lieutenant Harris immediately turned the patrol around but found some twenty or more coming from behind them. They were in a canyon with walls too steep for the horses to climb so the only alternative was to head to some boulders about a hundred yards away. The scout looked at the boulders and the Comanche coming from their right and knew it was going to be a close race. A few seconds later both the Calvary troop and the Comanche met just as they reached the boulders.

The scout and maybe half the men made in inside the circle of Boulders. They watched in horror as the remaining men that didn't make it were killed, some by the eight-to-ten-foot spears carried by some of the warriors and others heads were bashed by tomahawk blows or were knifed by warriors leaping from their ponies back and knocking the soldiers off their ponies. The scout, Amos Lind, looked at the terrified faces of the remaining soldiers who for the most part had not even fired a shot and he knew they were doomed. The Comanche rode away from the boulders to where the larger group had halted.

"What do you think Amos?"

"Make peace with the Lord Lieutenant," he answered. "Here they come," he shouted. He looked at the troops. "Use your damn weapons."

They fired their seven shot Spenser's. Only warriors Amos seen fall were the ones he shot and then the Comanche were leaping off their ponies and leaping over the boulders to get at the soldiers. The scout saw the men brutally butchered. An arrow had hit the Lieutenant in the throat, and he was dying, blood gurgling from his lips. Amos grabbed the officer's side arm and scrambled deeper into the boulders hoping he would not be seen. An arrow had hit him in the left shoulder as he scrambled away but with all the adrenalin flowing he didn't pay much attention to it. Sitting in the shadows of the boulders he quickly reloaded the Colts and kept his head down. That's when the pain hit him, and he almost screamed but bit his lip and took a quick look at the tip of the arrow that protruded from his shoulder.

He could hear the Comanche laughing as they scalped the troops and one trooper must have been alive because he heard a terrible scream, much to the delight of the warriors. The next thing he heard was the sound of horses leaving. He waited the three hours till almost dusk before he painfully stood up and looked around. He almost vomited at what he saw. Most of the men were not recognizable due to the butchery by the Comanche. He had seen the aftereffects of other battles before, but this butchery he had never saw before. Eyes were cut out, noses and ears cut off, hands were cut off some of the men and other vile things done. *These had to be very angry warriors to take the time to do this*, he thought. He found a dead horse and took the canteen and saddle bags. He gathered up probably twenty or shells for his Spenser and put them into the bags along with some jerky he found. His shoulder hurt like holy hell, but he knew his only chance to live would be to make it to the fort. It was only about forty or so miles, but in his condition it would seem a lot longer. He decided to travel at night and hole up during the day. He should make it day after tomorrow. It was now dark, so he started walking.

The Comanche band were in a good mood. The killing of the blue coats and all the scalps taken made them forget the trap earlier by the bluecoats from Clark that is all of them with the exception of Quanah. He was deeply troubled that he had been outsmarted by the soldiers from

Clark and especially the scout, Watkins! He spit when he mentioned his name. He had watched when he jumped up with his knife and tomahawk and cut his braves down like so many trees.

"He is all that I have heard he was. The next time I will not underestimate him and I will outsmart the great scout. "

"What are you saying?" Little Bear asked.

Quanah, realizing he was talking out loud to himself in English answered. "I was just talking to myself about what I was going to do to Watkins."

"I saw what he did to our brothers that were among the bluecoats this morning. If not for him we would have many more scalps. He is a warrior to respect."

" Maybe," Quanah said, "But that will not stop me from killing and scalping him and taking his family as captives." He smiled when he thought of that.

~~

It took a little longer to get to Fort Clark than Tye had expected. Stopping a few times to care for the wounded was time consuming, but necessary. When close to the fort he asked the Lieutenant if he could ride ahead and report to Thurston and have the medical people waiting. Harrison had told him he thought it was a good idea, so Tye nudged Sandy and was off at a gallop.

Arriving at the fort Tye immediately went to Thurston's office. Thurston heard his orderly acknowledge Tye and Thurston was out of his chair and met Tye in the outer office.

"Come into my office and tell me what is going on. Oh, by the way good to see you," he said shaking his scout's hand."

"Good news, bad news Sir. The good news we licked the Comanche pretty good with only six killed and eight wounded including Lieutenant Jameson who caught an arrow in his thigh. Before I give you the bad news I want you to know that I think both Lieutenant Jameson and Lieutenant Harrison are going to make fine officers. Neither think they know everything and are open to suggestions from veterans. That's a good sign for me and the other scouts."

"Thanks for that Tye. God knows we need more good officers out here. And the bad?"

"After the fight I along with Harrison met with Quanah. He's pissed that we outsmarted him and then ambushed him. He had his men pick up the dead that we had laid out and headed back north. Before he left he said he would be back with five hundred warriors or more and kill every person in the fort and take their families captive.

"MY GOD"! Thurston said loud enough the orderly came rushing in thinking he needed something. Thurston sent him back to his desk by the front door. "Do you think he was serious?"

"As sure as I am standing here Sir. I think we may have two weeks or so to make plans before he is back."

Thurston walked to his office window that looked over the parade ground and stood there for a moment with his hands clasped behind his back. He turned and walked back to his desk and sat down. "Treat me the same way you treat officers in the field. What do you think we need to do?"

Tye sat down. "Well Sir, first of all I have seen too many soldiers and officers killed the last few years including some three days ago because if they don't have a rifle or Colt in their hands they are pretty much helpless. I would like to immediately start training your officers and sergeants in hand-to-hand fighting with knives and tomahawks. They in turn can help train the men. I know we can improve their chances of survival if we do this. Now to the problem at hand. I know with your patrols out you have what, 120 or so men at the fort at any one time?"

"Pretty close to that number. What about the sabers the men carry?"

Tye laughed. "About as useful as tits on a boar hog. In close combat use you are going to inches or maybe a foot from the enemy. The only use for the sword they carry is if you have room for a full slashing motion. The point is rounded and not good for thrusting. I would like your permission to have the forts two blacksmith to convert them into about ten-inch knives and I would like to give the men lessons on how to use them."

Thurston nodded. You are right about the sword being pretty useless now that I think about it. I'll talk to the smiths.

"You remember a couple years ago when Captain McClelland joined the Apaches led by Yahzie to fight off a large band of Comanche led by Parker?"

He chuckled, "Yes. I caught some lip from Washington over that."

"Well hold on to your butt Sir because I want to talk to Yahzie to see if he will join us this time to fight the Comanche. He knows if he wipes us out his people will be next."

"We are still having some trouble with the Apaches."

"Yes Sir we are, but they are not from Yahzie's branch of the Lipan. They are from the ones a little farther south led by Juh."

"How many warriors do you think Yahzie could round up?"

"Not sure Sir, but it would be more fighting men than we have now."

"When do you plan to do this?"

I would like to take McClelland with me tomorrow if he is available. I'm going to see Rebecca and the kids now. The troops should be here pretty soon. You might have old sawbones ready to doctor them up." With that said he walked out.

~~

Up north, Amos Lind layup resting after walking all night. His shoulder was paining him something fierce and he knew he had to do something. He decided to take a chance on a small fire surrounded by rocks. He took his knife and carefully cut the shaft just below the point leaving him enough of the shaft to grab hold of. Grasping the shaft with his right hand he took a deep breath and jerked hard. The shaft, feathers ad all slipped from his shoulder. He almost passed out, but he knew the worse was to come. He lay his knife in the small fire and left it there till the blade was glowing red. There was nothing he could do about the hold in the back, but he could stop the bleeding in front and just hoped the blood in the back stopped on its own. When the knife was glowing he again took a deep breath and quickly laid the blade on the skin next to the hole and moved it across the exit wound melting the skin across it. He passed out.

When he awoke the fire was out and looking at the sun figured in mid-morning. He sat up and noticed right away his shoulder was not throbbing anymore but still hurt like hell. There was nothing he could do about it, so he ate some jerky, drank a small amount of water and lay back hoping to get some sleep.

~~

Back at Fort Clark, Tye was enjoying time with Rebecca, the kids and Buff. They were sitting in the shade of a large tree beside Los Moras Creek that ran in front of their home.

Rebecca asked. "You glad to be back scouting again instead of chasing outlaws?"

Tye Laughed and answered. "One of the soldiers asked me that question a couple days ago."

Rebecca waited and then said, "Well?"

"Told him I didn't know how much I missed getting up at four in the morning, eating hardtack, and riding with a bunch of smelly soldiers," he answered chuckling.

Buff asked. "How long yu gonna be heer Sunny? It's kinda nice yu being heer so this ole man don't hafta to be daddee and gramps tu. That sorter wares a man down yuh no," and he laughed along with Tye and Rebecca.

Tye explained all that happened the last two days including Quanah's threat. He also said he and Captain McClelland were going to find Yahzie tomorrow and see what he thinks and if he might be willing to help.

Rebecca pulled Nicole and Little Ben close to her. "Do you think he was serious about coming back?"

"I've got to plan like he is. He's come down twice in the last two years and got his tail run back north both times. I think he will come to save face with his people. I know I would if I was in his place."

"Sum men ar cuming Tye," Buff said looking over Tye's shoulder.

Tyr turned to see Major Thurston, Captain McClelland, and lieutenant Bullis. "This looks like trouble coming," Tye commented.

Tye stood up. "What's up Major? Looks like you have the war department with you."

Everyone shook hands paid their respects to Rebecca. Bullis spoke first. "Tye, you know Lieutenant Alexander don't you." Tye nodded. "Well, he was on patrol south of here along the Rio Grande. Two of his men, badly wounded, made it back to the fort about an hour ago. They were ambushed by a large group of Apaches yesterday morning. Alexander and the rest of the patrol were either killed or captured. They said the scout said he recognized Juh before he was killed."

McClelland spoke up. "We're thinking it was near where you was raised and we figured since you know that area like the back of your hand we could maybe pick your brain."

"Why pick my brain," Tye said. "Get a damn patrol together and I'll take you there and find that sonof....." He looked at Rebecca. "Sorry Honey. That sorter slipped out."

Rebecca laughed. "I've heard worse from you before." She looked at Major Thurston. "Guess you will want him in the morning. He will probably scare the horses with his smelly clothes since I have not had time to wash them. If you men will excuse me I need to get some things ready for him." She took the kids and went into the house.

Major Thurston said. "You are a lucky man Tye. Not many men could find a woman like that. McClelland and Bullis nodded in agreement.

"I'll get a patrol ready for in the morning," Thurston said. Lieutenant Bullis will lead the patrol with some of his Seminole scouts."

"Did the patrol with Harrison get back, Sir?'

"About two hours ago. They were pretty messed up. Most will be laid up for a week or so."

"How is Sergeant Arnold?"

"He is tougher than nails Tye. Says he's ready to ride again," Thurston said shaking his head. "Why?"

"Since I'm going to be gone for a day or two or more we have to be doing something about Quanah. McClellan and Arnold know Yahzie and he them. Maybe they could explain the situation to him and see what he says."

"A good idea Tye," McClellan said and looked at Thurston.

Thurston thought for a moment. Then nodded. "I'll get with Arnold and will see that four more men can go with you." He looked at Tye. "I know you trust Yahzie, but I am not sure I do enough to send just two men." *If Yahzie want to kill two men he would kill six just as easy,* Tye thought but kept his thoughts to himself.

Tye looked at Bullis. "Guess I'll see you in the morning Lieutenant." And shook all three men's hands.

Chapter Six

Before daylight the next morning found Tye saying goodbye to his family. He walked the short distance to the stables to get Sandy but found Bullis, four Seminole Scouts and a troop of twenty men waited. Sandy was saddled and waiting.

"Good afternoon Tye," Bullis said laughing.

Tye shrugged. "Saying goodbye to my family Lieutenant. Are we ready to move out?"

Tye led them across Los Moras Creek and then west on the Old Road for a short distance and then turned off the road and headed south. The scouts rode up to him and introduced themselves: Sergeant John Ward, Private Pompey Factor, and Trumpeter Isaac Payne.

Author's note: All three of the scouts were later awarded the Medal of Honor for their heroic action on April 25th, 1875, in saving Lieutenant Bullis from a band of Comanche. Their graves along with many other Seminole Scouts and their families can be seen today at the Seminole Cemetery in the southwest corner of Fort Clark.

While riding in front of the command the scouts and Tye were in conversion about everything from reading sign, sign language to fighting with knives. The one thing the Negro scouts learned quickly was that there was not one iota of bigotry in Tye's body. All men in his eyes are the same regardless of color of skin. When Tye rode ahead to scout along with Ward, Factor and Payne rode on the right and left flanks about three hundred yards out.

Later Tye and Ward rode into the yard of an old, abandoned homestead. Tye excused himself and walked to two graves and knelt between them. "I know it's been a while since I was here to visit with you. Things have been a little hectic with me chasing outlaws and now back to scouting. Rebecca and the kids are fine and old Buff is… well just dependable loving Buff. He still talks in that old mountain man's lingo that for some people, well they just cannot figure out what he is talking about. Little Ben is four now and growing like a tree. Probably going to be bigger than me. Nicole is as pretty as a picture just like her mother." The sound of the troops arriving caught Tye's attention. He stood up, his back to the troops and his eyes misting over said, "I gotta go. Just wanted you to know I think of you every day and I love ya'll and I miss you." He stood for a moment longer till the mist dried up and walked over to Sandy, mounted and rode away.

"Whut wus that all abut, Sir? Ward asked Bullis.

"This is where Tye was born and raised," Bullis answered. "If I was guessing, I'd say that's his parent's graves. Now go catch up with him."

Tye saw the buzzards ahead and from the number of them he knew that was where the ambush was. Riding in he and the scout scattered the damnable birds. When Ward suggested they just fire a couple of shots to scare them away. Tye explained they would scatter but any Apache within a mile or so would hear the shots.

"Stay here for a minute please," Tye said. "Let me look around some." It was Apache work all right, butchery one could not imagine, and the buzzards had only made it worse. When he heard the troops coming he hollered over to Ward to keep them back for a few more minutes.

Tye, after reading sign and looking at the tracks walked over to where Bullis and the troops were.

"About forty or fifty of them Sir. They came from around that rise over there in an all-out charge. I doubt most of the men had a chance to fire more than one shot before it was over with. They never had a chance Sir!"

"Damn!" Bullis shouted. "Where was the scout? I don't see his body anywhere."

"Come with me Sir." Bullis and Ward followed to some boulders. "He put up a hell of fight Sir. There must be twenty shell casings lying around him. Do you two notice anything else?"

Bullis was quiet but Sergeant Ward spoke up. "His body ain't cut up none."

"That's right. Apaches don't mutilate a warrior. This man was a warrior. Don't know how many he hit with those bullets but I'm betting it was more than few. I'm betting the

two that escaped did so while they were trying to get to him."
Tye mounted Sandy. "The Apache are across the river into
Mexico. I would suggest we need to take the dead back and
bury them at the fort. Bullis reluctantly agreed knowing they
could not cross the Rio Grande and go into Mexico without
causing a real problem with Mexico.

~~

Way to the north, scout Lind was about five miles
from Fort Concho. He figured being this close to the fort no
Comanche would be around, so he continued walking, rather
stumbling forward. He knew his shoulder was infected
because he waited too long to get the arrow out plus probably
some of the feathers came off when he pulled the shaft out
but what was done was done. He was only half conscious
when he felt hands on his shoulders. Instinctually he jerked
away and drew his Colt.

"Amos, its Lieutenant Jonas from Fort Concho."

Lind   stood there swaying back and forth with his
gun pointed toward the Lieutenant and two other soldiers.
Finally, after a tense few seconds he dropped the Colt and
collapsed to the ground unconscious. Two soldiers rushed
and picked him up and carried him to a huge boulder that
was reasonable flat on top and gently lay him across it. The

Lieutenant poured water from his canteen on Lind's face waking him up.

"What happened Lind?" Where's the patrol and Lieutenant Harris?"

Lind painfully and with the help of one of the troopers sat up. "I need a drink of water Lieutenant. Haven't had any since yesterday morning." After drinking the water, he said. "Dead Sir. All of them. We were ambushed by maybe seventy or eighty Comanche. I think I glimpsed Quanah leading them. I was in the rocks with the men that were not killed right off along with Lieutenant Harris when we were overrun and the men panicked, with some of them dropping their weapons trying to surrender. Harris was beside me and took an arrow in the throat. I turned to get farther in the rocks when an arrow hit me in the back of the shoulder, and I crawled farther in them. For some unknown reason they either forgot about me or didn't see me I don't know which, but when I woke up it was almost dark. I knew I had to get to the fort with what happened and the onliest chance I had to get there was to travel by night and rest during the day. That was two days ago…I think."

The lieutenant nodded and asked, "Can you ride?"

"Just get me on a horse Lieutenant." After giving directions as where the ambush took place the patrol left to see about the dead and Lind, along with another trooper headed back to Fort Concho.

~~

Thirty minutes after heading back to Fort Clark Tye held up his hand and Bullis stopped the patrol. Bullis and Ward rode up to where Tye was waiting.

"What do you see on the ground?" Both men leaned forward and looked where Tye was pointing.

"I don't see anything but some shod pony tracks, ours from earlier," Bullis said.

John dismounted for a closer look. After looking for a few seconds he stood up. "Lordy. Sir, a whole passel of Indians crossed here from the west."

"Yep. There took some time with brush to try and wipe out their tracks and just leave ours. Did a heck of a job to."

"We were moving pretty fast Tye so how did you see them?" Bullis asked.

"Lieutenant, it is important for a scout to know. Don't get your mind set on one thing. Keep your eyes moving and look for little things that are out of place. See those bushes over there on the north side of the road. The Apache tried to put them in a hole and stand up but two have fallen over. I was curious so I went over to take a closer look and found several that were not rooted in. Walked over to the west side and found where they had been pulled up and put two and two together. About fifty or more crossed here. I'm betting it was Juh and his bunch that have come back.

"What are you thinking?" Bullis asked.

Tye thought for a moment before answering. "If it's okay with you, take a break and give the scouts and men and horses a few minutes to rest up. I'll take the Sergeant here and follow the tracks to see what I can find out. See those boulders over there. If you hear shots being fired and see two men riding like the devil is after them take your men there and get ready to meet Juh."

Bullis nodded. "Take care, both of you."

"Always do Lieutenant," Tye replied smiling and rode off with the Seminole Scout, Sergeant Ward.

Twenty minutes later they were riding like hell with about twenty Apaches chasing them. The Apache came out of the brush almost on top of them and were now only fifty or so yards behind them. Tye turned and fired his Colt three time because it was louder than the rifle he had hoping the lieutenant heard them. They were a quarter of a mile from the rocks when he heard John grunt. He turned and saw the scout falling from his horse. Reacting quickly, he grabbed the man by the back of his neck and lifted him back in the saddle and held him there. This slowed them some and Tye knew the race to the rocks was going to be close. They were forty yards out when rifles blasted from the rocks and half of the Apaches hit the hard rocky ground. Three or four more were slumped over their ponies back as they turned and rode about three hundred yards away and stopped. Bullis saw one of the Apaches ride away.

Tye reined in Sandy and three soldiers came out to help Ward down from his horse. Ward grabbed Tye's hand. "Thanks Tye. I owe you my life."

Tye smiled. "You may not be thanking me later when I cut that arrow out the back of your shoulder." Ward tried to smile but failed miserably.

Tye looked around where they were. "Not the best to place to defend but not the worse."

"What happened?" Bullis asked.

The Apaches come around a bend in the road and were as surprised as we were. We reversed our direction and rode as hard and fast as we could. Ward got hit with an arrow about a quarter mile away from you. Slowed us some with me having to hold him in the saddle but we made it."

"What now?"

"I suspect we are going to have a passel of visitors Lieutenant. Better tell your men what to expect and get their ammo from their saddle bags and also their canteens and get ready to earn their thirteen dollars a month."

While Bullis was telling his men what Tye had said, Tye was looking at Wards wound. The tip of the arrowhead was barely pushing the skin up but not breaking the skin on his chest. *Damn*, he thought. *This is going to hurt him more than I thought. At least I think it missed his lung*, he thought when seeing no bloody froth around Wards lips. At that instant he heard the sound of a lot of horses, so he pulled Wards limp body behind some rocks and scrambled up beside Bullis.

"GIVE THEM HELL MEN!" he shouted and was immediately follow by a volley from the soldiers with their recently issued seven shot Spencer's. Tye knocked one off the back of his pony and noticed that there were several ponies with no riders which pleased him. *They have been trained well,* he thought as he knocked another from the back of his pony. The men fired another volley from their Spencer's and several more ponies had no riders. But, the Apache had let loose with two volley of arrows and even from horseback they have been trained to be pretty accurate and several found soft flesh. The second volley from the soldiers Colts had turned the charge and they were regrouping three hundred yards away. At this time the other Comanche joined their brothers making their total an over whelming advantage.

Bullis shouted. "Sergeant Anderson, Give me a casualty report."

"Yes Sir." A few minutes later the report came. "Five dead eight wounded of which four can still fight."

"Damn!" Bullis muttered under his breath. "Almost half my command are dead are wounded."

'They lost about twenty or so Sir. I think they will be hesitant to charge again real soon which will give us a little time to look at the wounded. I think I will give them something to think about. Tye rested his elbow on the rock and aimed just above the head of one of the nearest warriors and slowly stroked the trigger of his Henry repeater. He rifle bucked against his shoulder and all watched as a warrior tumbled off his pony. The others retreated farther away but not fast enough as Tye fired again and watched as another slump over his ponies back much to the pleasure of the men.

"Your men have been well trained Lieutenant. There a lot of Apache lying out there and I'm betting there are more not feeling too good."

"I work the men pretty hard. Would like to have more time on the shooting range but the people in Washington are too damn cheap thinking we would waste bullets if they were readily available." He spit on the ground when he said, "Damn politicians!"

Tye nodded his agreement and stood up. "Going to see to the wounded Sir." He started with the Seminole Scout, Ward. Ward lying on his side because of the arrow in his back was awake. Tye wished he was still passed out. "Lieutenant, can you have a man to assist me and someone to start a fire." Tye put his knife in the fire long enough to sterilize it. He picked up a small stick and told Ward to bite down on this because this is going to hurt like hell. Taking his knife, he cut the skin where the point was pushing out the skin on Ward's shoulder.

Tye pushed the arrow from the back through and out the front. He then cut the flint tip off the shaft and moving behind Ward he told the trooper helping him to hold his shoulder. Tye then jerked hard, and the arrow slipped from Wards shoulder. He looked at Ward. Lots of sweat was running down his face and the stick he held in his teeth lay on the ground in two pieces.

" I know it hurts like hell Sergeant but what I have to do now is going to do the same. He took the knife that was glowing red from the fire and melted the flesh over the hole in the front and back of the shoulder. Ward never uttered a word but passed out. Tye doctored the others the best he could but two had arrows that could not be removed in the field. They were moved farther back in the rocks and given their Colts in case they were over run so they could fight to protect themselves. In the circle of rocks there was Tye, Bullis, and six healthy men and four wounded but would still be able to fire their rifles. It was not a good situation for the patrol since they were facing maybe forty or so Apache warriors.

"Are we good as dead Tye?"

"Hell, no Lieutenant. Not as long as there is blood flow through our veins." Tye stood and faced the men. They all looked at him. "I know you men are scared. I am too. I've stayed alive out here with no telling how many skirmishes I have been in over the years with Apaches and bandits. You can get through this too if you do what I have learned. You have to decide if you want to live and if you do you have to make up your mind and tell yourself I am the meanest damn sonofabitch on earth and today ain't my day to die. Fire your rifles till they are empty and then use them as clubs. Fight, fight for yourself, fight for you buddy next to you, and fight to get back to your loved ones. Don't give up men. The Calvary seldom is in a fight where they are not outnumbered. You just have to want to live. DO YOU WANT TO LIVE? Tye shouted the question.

A loud chorus of yells one louder than the others. Tye picked him out. "You there," and pointed him out, "Have to be a southern boy."

"Sure, as hell proud to be an ole boy from Alabama."

"Fight in the War?"

"Hell yes. Served with Lewis in the Alabama Calvary!"

"I thought that was a rebel yell I heard. I had an encounter a couple years ago with some ex-confederate soldiers and they were meaner than hell. I expect for you to show these men how a rebel fights for his life."

"Hell yes! Count on me Tye."

"That was quite a speech," Bullis quietly commented.

"HERE THEY COME!" ONE OF THE TROOPERS SCREAMED.

The quietness was suddenly broken by shouts of the men, screams of the charging Apaches, and the sounds of guns blasting through it all. Tye heard the familiar rebel yell above all of it and smiled and then his 13 shot Henry opened up. Several Apaches ponies were rider less from the soldiers and Tye's fire. Most of the Apaches turned their charge but several left their ponies backs and leaped on the soldiers with knives and tomahawks.

Tye saw one trooper go down and then the soldiers screaming like bloody maniacs leapt at the warriors swinging their Spencer's like clubs. Tye and Bullis waded in, Bullis with his sword and Tye with his knife and tomahawk. Both were screaming also. Bullis took a glancing blow to the head from a club and went down. Tye straddled the lieutenant and swinging both the tomahawk and his Bowie kept the Apaches off Bullis. It was over in a less than a minute. Bullis had come to and realized Tye was above him with his tomahawk and knife dripping blood and realized his life had been saved by this giant of a man.

The troopers were congratulating each other when Tye shouted, "Reload your guns. They will be back." He knelt down to check on Bullis. "How's the head?"

"Hurts like hell," he replied. "Thanks."

"For what?"

"I came around in time to see you keeping the Apache off me."

"I was just protecting myself."

"Yeah, of course you were. Thanks again anyway."

Tye knelt down and looked at Bullis's head. He took the lieutenants kerchief and wrapped in around the lieutenants' head. "Hell Sir, that's just a scratch. Best you get comfortable behind the boulder again."

"You really think they will be back?" Bullis asked looking at all the dead Apaches lying in the dirt.

"As sure as I'm standing here only this time they will be a little smarter." He left to check on the men. He saw the kid from Alabama. "Hey Rebel. What's the casualty report?"

"One dead and one wounded but he can still fight," Tye.

"Check your weapons again. One of you come over here with the lieutenant and myself."

A private jumped up and ran over to them. "Get behind that boulder over there on the other side of the lieutenant and watch the area to our right. The land on the left broke off steeply and would take a horse a while to get up which would endanger the rider. Tye figured Juh had seen that and would split his men and come in from the front and from the west, Tye and the men's left.

"Look men, I know I am no officer or even a sergeant but listen to me." Tye nudged Bullis and both men listened to the young rebel. "These damned Apaches know we only have a few men able to fight and they have us outnumbered what…four or five to one? What they don't know is that as desperate men in a desperate situation is just mean and dangerous as a rattlesnake. Are we going to show them?" he yelled.

"Hell yes we are," they all answered and waved their Spencer's above their heads.

"You ought to make him a sergeant Lieutenant."

"I will do that Tye, if we get out of this mess."

"Here they come," Tye shouted.

As Tye figured they came from two directions, head on and from the west. Tye, Bullis, and a private Kelly cut loose on the ones from the west and the others were shooting with deadly accuracy on the Apaches coming from the front. Tye was firing his Henry as fast as he could pull the trigger. Bullis and Kelly were firing their seven shot Spencer's when Tye and Bullis heard an arrow hitting flesh and Kelly was down, an arrow protruding from the back of his neck. Tye emptied his Henry and drew his Colt. Bullis had already drawn his.

Suddenly it was over as quickly as it began. The Apache withdrew with heavy losses. Tye walked among the battle-weary troopers, some in a daze. He counted three dead counting Kelly and two wounded pretty bad and may not make it. He was glad to see the Alabama boy on his feet apparently not wounded.

"What's your name?" Tye asked the young rebel.

"Gary Garner."

Tye was taken back a couple years to another soldier by that name who had been killed. He was a friend of Tye's and a hell of a soldier. "Do you have any relatives out here?"

"None that I know. Why?"

"I guess it's just a consequence but there was a Sergeant Gary Garner here that was a friend of mine. He was killed a couple years ago by the Apache."

"Sorry to hear that Tye, but he wasn't a relative I knew of."

"Can you help me with the wounded?"

"Yes Sir." Tye patched up the ones he could but the two with arrows in the chest was a different matter. They were in a place of few trees so that eliminated making travois they could lie on behind a horse. Tye told Bullis they would have to ride double and didn't think they would make it to Clark."

Bullis nodded. "Do you think the Apache are gone?"

"Yes Sir. They took a pretty good licking Sir. I think they are going back to Mexico. There will be enough wives and mothers now that will be wailing and cutting their hair over the loss of husbands and sons." Tye looked around. We still have some daylight left. I think we need to get things together and put some distance from here in case I am wrong."

From what Bullis had seen the last two days he doubted Tye was wrong. They put the dead, wrapped in blankets along with the dead troopers from yesterday on horses. The wounded were helped on to theirs. Tye cut the shafts off as short as possible so the two with chest wounds could ride double, tied to the man in front to keep them from falling off.

When they moved out Tye said to Bullis after looking back at what was left of the patrol. "We are a sorry looking lot Sir but I'm proud of every damn one of them…soldiers all."

Chapter Seven

They were a raggedy looking bunch as they rode into Brackett and crossed the bridge over Los Moras Creek and entered Fort Clark. Both of the men with wounds in the chest had died making the total eight dead and only Tye, Privates Bailey and Garner escaped with no serious wounds. When they reached headquarters Captain Anderson, the Post Surgeon, met them and ushered the wounded to the hospital while Tye and Bullis met with Major Thurston.

Lieutenant Bullis reported everything to Thurston including his recommendation for Private Garner for promotion. Bullis said, "If not for Tye and Garner giving his speech encouraging the men we would not be here. I would like to add that I would not be here at all if not for Tye standing over me when I went down and killing Apaches that were trying to get to me. Also, off the record, I would like to say I will add to the stories I have heard about him," he said laughing.

"That goes for every man who has ridden with him. I know we are lucky to have him back on the payroll as Chief Scout," Thurston said. "Lieutenant, go to the hospital and let Captain Anderson look at that head wound and then get some rest."

"Have you heard from Captain McClelland?" Tye asked.

"Not yet but I figure we will maybe tonight or in the morning at the latest."

"Well then," Tye said, "I think I will mosey down to the house and surprise my family. Let me know when you hear from McClellan."

~~

Thirty miles northwest of Fort Clark, Captain McClellan and Sergeant Arnold was heading back to the fort after a festive meeting with Yahzie. Yahzie and his people were happy to see the two soldiers and had a feast for them remembering their help in sending the raiding Comanche back north several moons ago. They feasted on venison, corn which was probably stolen from a Mexican village and various berries. The men and women danced till late when everyone returned to their wickiup. Yahzie, knowing if they did not help the bluecoats and the Comanche killed the troops at Clark they would be fighting them alone. They agreed that Yahzie would keep a brave by the place where the Pecos met the Rio Grande to await the signal from the bluecoats that the Comanche were headed their way.

~~

Days like today were the happiest of Tye's life: playing with Little Ben and Nicole and hanging around the house with Rebecca and Buff. He and Buff were sitting on the Porch with the two kids while Rebecca was fixing something to eat for lunch. Buff as he was fixing to be seventy-seven years of age and for the first time was talking about some things he had never mentioned to Tye.

"Yu kno Tye I have lived a long time. A lot mor'n than most uf my frends frum tha days in tha Rockie Montons. Sumtimes I wuld like ta kno if frends like Bridger and ole Stumpee were still aroun and above ground. I kno my days ar numbr'd and afo'r I tak my last breth I wud like ta kno." I

done told ya th I nev'r had no famlee at leest none I kno uf.
I jus don't kno jus how much my time heer with yu, Rebecca
and tha kids hav meent ta me. Liv'n heer in a house and
und'r a roof fer tha ferst tim sence I was a kid at home. Liv'd
in cav's and teepees most my soree life.But yak kno, I don't
thank I wud chane anee thang if'n I cud. Liv'd my life tha
way I wanted ta. Didn't anser ta no one. Tho't I wus tha
happest I cud be but tha last few yeers here, with ya'll sho'd
me jus how much I mist out on." He didn't say anything for
a moment because his eyes misted over, and he was a little
choked up.

Tye put his arm around the little man and hugged
him. "Whatever joy we have brought to you Buff, it doesn't
compare to the joy and comfort you have brought to me,
Rebecca, and the kids. You will never know how much a
comfort it is to me when I'm away that you are here to take
care of my wife and kids. You are family. I'll get the major
to inquire about your friends."

Rebecca came out of the house. "Kids are asleep for
a while. She sat down on the other side of Buff and realized
she had interrupted something. She looked at Buff and the
tears and knew what they were talking about. It was not the
first time Buff had talked about the old days and the fact he

never married. She took Buff's hands in hers. "I don't think you realize how much you mean to this family old man. The kids worship you and Tye and I love you more than anything."

"Lootenant Harrison's kuming", Buff said.

"Morning Ty, Buff." He took his hat off and bowed slightly to Rebecca. "Morning to you too Ma'am." He turned to Tye. "Major wanted me to tell you that McClellan and Sergeant Arnold arrived about thirty minutes ago and request your presence at his office."

Tye stood up. "See you two in a little while," and left with the Lieutenant.

Arriving at headquarters they were ushered in by the orderly. Both McClelland and Sergeant Arnold were standing in front of the major's desk. Tye shook hands with both men. "Did you meet Yahzie?"

McClelland spoke. "Had a good talk with him Tye. He knows they will be next if the Comanche defeat us. He is keeping a man on the Mexican side of the river where the Brazos and the river meet to await a message that the Comanche are coming. He asked if you would come to him to discuss some plan of attack."

"Of course," Tye replied, "Just as soon as the Major, McClelland, Harrison and myself come up with one. There's another thing I wanted to discuss with you Major."

"What's that, Tye?"

"I've seen a lot of soldiers die the last few years Major. A lot of them unnecessarily."

Thurston sat down at his desk and motioned Tye to sit also. "Explain."

"Soldiers do fine when they have their rifles and Colts to keep the Apache or Comanche at a distance but they ain't worth a tinker's damn in a close hand to hand combat situation. Not all of course, some are just natural, but the majority is at a loss in a knife fight. What I propose is to teach them how to handle a knife, how to survive. I firmly believe that if they are at least somewhat capable of handling a knife their odds surviving increase."

I would like to start with the scouts and the officers and they in turn can help me with the troops. I figure the Seminole scouts are probably proficient, but I don't know. I know your scout Bowlegs and my friend Dan is more than capable."

When do you want to start? And what about knives? Most of the men don't have one big enough to help them."

"For the most part the saber they carry is good for one thing, to make a lot of racket when riding a horse. I could get the blacksmith to make a hell of a knife out of one. Get the post blacksmith and the one in Brackett and we can have a lot of them in a week or so. In the meantime, I can make a couple out of wood for the men to use for practice."

"Do you really think it will help?"

"I'm living proof Major. My pa made damn sure I knew the ins and outs of knife fighting and it's more than once saved me."

"Let's do it then," Thurston said standing up. "First thing in the morning. I'll set things up with First Sergeant O'Malley to have all available men on the parade ground."

"Thanks Major. I'll get Buff to help me carve some knives out this afternoon and tonight."

Tye left and headed toward his home. Arriving, he explained his plan to Buff.

"Tha shor can't hurt them thar solgurs nune. Might jus save sum uf thar soree asses," he chuckled. They got busy whittling. By the time they went to bed they had six pretty fair knives whittled out with eight-inch blades.

The next morning First Sergeant O'Malley had forty soldiers on the parade field whom not a one had any idea why they were there since they were not marching in formation.

"Gather round men. Today is the first day of your training in hand-to-hand combat with knives. After the lesson this morning I want you to turn your sabers in to the post blacksmith. Which of you can handle a knife? Three men raised their hands. "You men step forward." Tye handed the largest of the three a wooden knife. "You are in a fight with the Comanche, which you will be in a few days, and you have emptied your Spencer and your Colt, and you are face to face with a Comanche warrior. What do you do?"

The man just stood there. "DAMMITT MAN! WHAT DO YOU DO? I am a Comanche warrior, and I am fixing to kill you. The man dropped into a crouch and took a wild swing at Tye. Tye stepped back and sliced the blade of his wooden knife across the man's forearm as it passed by. The big man raised the knife above his head and sliced down trying to hit Tye in the neck or shoulder. Tye caught the man's wrist and held it in a vice like grip as he tapped the man's belly with his blade. Tye let him go. The man charged like a bull buffalo and Tye grabbed his knife hand and falling to his back stuck his foot in the man's belly and then straighten out his leg as he fell backwards. The man did a somersault in the air landing hard on his back. When he opened his eyes, Tye was astride him with his blade on the man's neck.

He helped the man up. "I have watched too many soldiers die out here because without their rifle or Colt they are helpless. This is gonna change. Buff and me are going to put you through a quick survival course. You can or cannot take it serious, but it just might save you ass someday."

He looked at the men and then jumped toward them and let out a blood curdling scream. The men fell over themselves backing up. When everyone quit laughing, Tye said. "To survive a fight with an Apache or a Comanche you have to be as mean and vicious as they are. They will give you no mercy and will not expect any from you. Now pare off. He picked six men and gave each a knife. He then worked with each pair showing them how to stand, how to hold the knife and everything else his pa had taught him. Two hours later they left the parade ground and would be back in the morning to farther their "education." Tye and Buff would have another bunch in the afternoon.

Buff laughed. "You shor put tha feer of God in thos soldur boys when ya screemed like a damn Blackfut warrior. Reminded me uf yur pa jumpin up a screeming and swinging that thar tomeehawk in won hand and his knife in tha uther tha ferst time Bridger and me seed him fight. He wus a fighter Tye. Braveest man I ev'r did see.

The afternoon session was a repeat of the morning and would be the same every day for a week. By Friday evening Tye and Buff were sitting on the porch. "I feel we made some progress Buff. Maybe save a couple of them in the fight coming up."

"Yep! I kud see it in thar eyes."

"Well, let's enjoy the weekend and I will see the major first thing Monday morning."

Chapter Eight

Last week Major Thurston sent dispatch to riders to Fort Davis in the Davis Mountains and to Fort Concho near San Angelina (now San Angelo). The dispatches to George Andrews, Post Commander at Fort Davis and to Colonel Grierson at Fort Concho were short and to the point telling them to be alert for large band of Comanche under the war chief, Quanah Parker, that could be coming near them on their way south. If seen, please send dispatch rider to me here at Fort Clark.

Tye walked into Thurston's office early Monday before the major was there which was unusual since he was always there before the sun came up. He was standing looking at the wall map when Major Thurston walked in.

"Been thinking about what I need to tell Yahzie about our plan," Tye Said shaking hand with the major. "The problem is, we don't have a plan because we don't know when Quanah is coming, nor do we know what trail he will be on."

"So, what do we need to do?"

"Let me take my friend Dan August and a patrol north and find him. I can send Dan to Yahzie and a rider back here when we do."

"What if you miss him and we have no warning?"

"Five hundred or more Comanche are going to be hard to miss Major. There are only three trails he can use, and we can find him." He walked back over to the wall map. He pointed to Fort Davis. "The old Comanche war trail goes near Fort Davis, but that trail is the longer route to get here. He's not going to waste time that way. The other two ways take him on a more direct path from his stronghold in the Panhandle and will bypass Fort Concho. He's pissed Major so I'm betting he comes the direct route. Dan and I can split the patrol and he stays west of Concho and I will stay east. We won't miss him Sir."

"When do you figure on heading out?"

"As soon as I get the okay from you, Sir."

"I'll get a patrol ready if you can go to the Seminole scout camp and find August. I'll have the men ready in an hour."

"Dan and me will be ready." Tye went to the stable area and found Sandy. After saddling him he rode the half mile or so to the camp of the Seminole Scouts where he found Dan. After explaining the situation Dan said he would get his things together and meet Tye at headquarters. Tye rode to his home to get his things. He found Rebecca, the kids, and Buff on the porch with his clothes packed, rifle and knife and tomahawk.

"How did you know I was leaving?"

"Buff was at the O'Malley's when the soldier came and told him to get a patrol of fifteen men ready to leave immediately," Rebecca answered. "Since you were at headquarters I figured you were going to be scouting for the patrol."

"You are amazing," Tye said smiling. "That's why I love you so much." He picked up Nicole and Little Ben in his arms and hugged them. He then hugged and kissed Rebecca. He looked at Buff.

"Yu don't have ta say anee thang Tye. I'll watch over them." He stuck out his hand which Tye took and then Tye hugged the little man.

Tye picked up his things and gave Rebecca a kiss on the cheek. "Hopefully I won't be gone but three or four days." He mounted Sandy and rode toward headquarters. Arriving there he saw the troops ready to go. He spotted Dan and Lieutenant's Harrison and Bullis and he was especially pleased when he looked at the troops. He spotted Sargent Arnold, privates Bailey, Mason, Morley and O'Keefe. *All veterans that can be counted on in a pinch*, he thought to himself. *It's a dang good feeling to have men with you that you can trust to do their job.*

Far to the north Quanah had over four hundred warriors with him. Almost a hundred miles lay behind them to the canyon where their camp was where he left over a hundred warriors to protect it. They were traveling light with each brave carrying only their bows, arrows, knives, tomahawk and of course their favorite weapon, the eight-foot lance. They each had two gourds for water and a bag of pemmican to eat. Quanah had decided to go the direct route which would lead him to pass well east of Fort Concho. He wanted to stay clear of any patrols from the fort where would be spotted and possibly getting word to the Fort called Clark before they were ready to attack.

Tye and the patrol had left Brackett and traveled east for about twenty miles before turning north toward Fort Concho. There is a small mountain range north of Brackett which he knew would slow them down considerably. The mountains were not high but there were many places unpassable with cliffs and deep cuts that would have to be gone around. They were traveling fast stopping only to let their horses take a blow. By dusk they had traveled almost forty miles.

After making camp Tye looked at the six extra horses that he had requested. These would be used by the dispatch riders to get back to fort to report that Quanah had been spotted. Each would take three and alternate riding them. If none injured himself by stepping in a hole or pulling up lame a good rider that could read horses and knew how to get the most out of them without ruining them might cover eighty miles or more a day. This would mean they could get to Clark in a day and half giving plenty of time for the fort to prepare. Tye was pleased the hostler at the fort knew his business because the horses were exceptional, lean muscular build made for distance running and even had recently been shod.

Later, Tye and Lieutenants Harrison and Bullis squatted by their fire eating their supper of biscuits and bacon and washing them down with hot coffee.

Lieutenant Harrison asked. "When do you think we will be at Fort Concho Tye?"

Tye emptied his cup before speaking. "Maybe day after tomorrow. We still have about a hundred or so miles to go. About midday tomorrow we should be on level ground with lots of grass for the horses. We will push it a little more tomorrow and try to get fifty or sixty miles. Hopefully by tomorrow night's camp we will be only forty or so miles from the fort."

"Do you really think that he can muster five hundred braves?" Bullis asked.

"Don't know but I'm thinking he can. The Comanche, with the exception of maybe the Sioux, are the largest tribe I know of in numbers. Heard the Navajo have large numbers also. But as far as the best fighters the Comanche rates at the top of the list. The Apache would be there if they had the numbers, but they don't. That's the reason the Apache are down here because the Comanche overpowered them with their numbers and forced them farther and farther south. The Apache fight a hit and run war because of their fewer numbers and are damn good at it. He filled his cup again. "To answer your question Lieutenant, I think we are in for the fight of our lives in a few days." Tye threw the remains of his coffee on the ground. "I'm gonna get some sleep wile I can," and headed to his bed roll.

Harrison and Bullis watched him walk away and lay down. "After hearing what he said I don't think I want to close my eyes and go to sleep," Bullis said.

"I'm new out hear as you know so how long have you known Tye."

Long enough to know he knows Indians better any white man I know and the fact the Apache are a little scared of him tells you all you need to know about his fighting and tracking ability. I heard you witnessed some of his fighting ability."

"Yeah I did when we were being overrun in that canyon a while back. We were goners when he jumped up screaming like some crazy animal and charged right into the middle of them swinging his tomahawk and knife and cutting them down like we would trees. Comanche were falling right and left from his knife and tomahawk and the men took heart and started doing the same. After the Comanche left Sergeant Arnold came up to me and Tye and," he paused to laugh for a second, "He said damn Tye you must be getting old. You only killed seven of them and let some get away."

Bullis laughed. "Well Arnold is the man to talk to if you want to know about Tye. He has been on God know how many patrols and fights with the Apache with him. I know my Seminole scouts are pretty fierce themselves and they have nothing but respect for him. That alone tells me all I need to know about the man." He stood up and said, "I think it's a waste of time but I'm gonna try to get some rest. See you in three or four hours."

~~

Roughly one hundred miles to the north Quanah and his four hundred or so warriors sat around their campfires. Quanah was listening to his scouts excitingly reporting they had come across a camp of soldiers. When Quanah asked how many the scout held up both hands and spread his fingers two times. Listening he figured the camp was about four or five miles from this camp. He would attack it at daylight.

Five miles south of Quanah's camp Captain James Miles and Lieutenant Gary Simpson were talking about their families and the fact they had been on this patrol for five days and seen hide nor hair of any hostiles. They had come across a large number of unshod pony tracks, but they were headed north and were, according to their scout a week or so old. All the soldiers with the exception of their posted guards sat around their campfires completely unaware there were four hundred Comanche close by.

Captain Miles was a veteran of fifteen years and was highly regarded by the commander of Fort Concho. Besides that, he was liked by the troops, and they knew he would not get them unnecessarily killed by making a bad decision. He was thirty-five years old and married with two children who lived on the fort in the officers' quarters.

Miles, unlike his friend from west Point George Armstrong Custer, had no need for glory and admiration. He did his job and no more. His friend Custer would die along with all his men because of disobeyed orders and hunting glory in June 1876, two years from now. He worshipped his family and spent every spare minute with them. After talking for a few minutes more to Lieutenant Simpson he made the rounds checking the sentries and went to his bedroll.

Early the next morning a little before daylight the patrol prepared to leave. An excited entry came running in screaming COMANCHE! COMANCHE! Miles and Simpson ran to the edge of camp to look. A huge band of warriors were sitting on a hill three or four hundred yards away. Mile hollered for his scout and quickly scribble a message for him to take to the post commander.

Several hundred Comanche. Do not think we can outrun them but going to Try. They made be headed your way. May be four or five hundred.

He handed the message to the scout and told to get his ass out of here. "TO THE HORSES MEN. TAKE NOTHING EXCEPT YOUR WEAPONS, WATER AND AMMUNITION."

At that time the Comanche came storming toward them. The ground shook with the hooves of four hundred ponies and the air was filled with Comanche war cries. Miles, leading the escape knew they were in trouble when he saw forty or so to his right and in front. He began looking for a place to hole up that was defendable, but the land was treeless and flat with nothing but grass and sage brush and low hills occasionally. Suddenly he saw a dark spot on the land just in front of him, a large deep buffalo wallow. He turned toward it and the troops followed. He was gauging the distance to the wallow and the Comanche that was trying to cut him off. It was going to be close, real close. Looking over his shoulder at the great cloud of dust behind him he saw the main force were still a ways off.

Suddenly they were clambering down the walls of the wallow. Miles shouted. "EVERY FOURTH MAN TO THE HORSES. REST TO THE WALLS. It was too late. Before the men could scamper to the top of the wallow, Comanche warriors were off their ponies and leaping into the wallow and on top of the soldiers swinging their tomahawks and crushing skulls. Others stood on the crest of the wallow and shooting arrows into the men. Miles gathered what men were left and shooting their horses and laying down behind them started firing their carbines and Colts. Looking left and right of him Miles counted eleven men that were still able to fight.

An arrow in the throat took the man on his right which was Lieutenant Simpson. *"Yea thought I walk through th...*Miles did not finish the Lord's Prayer as an arrow struck him in the forehead as he looked over the back of his horse killing him instantly. He was one of the lucky ones. The rest of the men died with tomahawk bashes, and knives struck several times in their body as the warriors swept over them. A few were taken alive and suffered a horrible fate. When Quanah arrived, it was all over except the mutilation of the bodies and scalping.

When Quanah sat on his black pony and looked into the wallow all the men turned toward him and drew silent. He shouted, "We have a great victory here over the bluecoats here, but we must not forget our true purpose: the bluecoats at Fort Clark and the scout Watkins. We have vowed to kill them all for killing our brothers. Get to your ponies." Loud shouting followed as they raised their spears and war clubs and raced to their ponies some waving scalps.

~~

A day later Tye the troops arrived at Ft. Concho where he and Lieutenant Harrison met with the Post Commander, Colonel Grierson.

"Glad to see you again and especially to see that you still have your hair. You still on the Apache most wanted list?" he asked slapping Tye on the shoulder. The last time I met you was when you were chasing that scum El Diablo. Glad to hear you killed him."

"Yes Sir, he was a bad one. Sir this is Lieutenant Harrison from Clark." The two men shook hands.

"Sir, did you receive a dispatch from Major Thurston about Quanah Parker?" Lieutenant Harrison asked.

Grierson nodded his head. "Unfortunately, it came too late for me to get word to my patrol up north. Captain Miles, my best officer, is leading a twenty-man patrol. His scout came in last night with a message from Miles." He walked to his desk and picked up a piece of paper and handed it to the Lieutenant who read it and handed it to Tye.

"Have you heard anything since then from the patrol," Colonel?" Grierson lowered his head and shook it. "Sorry to hear that Colonel."

"I've got to send a patrol to find them."

"I know that is what needs to be done Colonel, but we are talking about four, possibly five hundred Comanche. Another patrol might meet them and be massacred also."

134

"So what do you think?"

"We are up here really as a scout patrol to see if what Quanah said to me after we killed a lot of his warriors and embarrassed him, "Tye Said. "Lieutenant Harrison here," he nodded toward Harrison, "and myself had a short Pow Wow with him after the fight. He said he would be back to kill every man, woman and child at Clark. I don't think this fort is in his plan for revenge. You might consider going ahead and make plans for an attack thought. Being prepared is better than being unprepared in this instance. If that large a force hit Fort Clark and we were unprepared it would be a disaster as it would here."

"Let me ask you a question Tye," Grierson Said. "What if, since Quanah is close, I give you and Lieutenant Harrison men to confront him. No telling how many homesteaders or other men and women who might be in their path who they would slaughter or torture to death on his way down to Clark.

"How many men could you send?"

'If I am certain they are not going to attack my fort I could give you almost one hundred men under yours and Harrison's command."

"I would like to speak to your men and explain the situation and then ask for volunteers if that is okay with you."

"I'll gather them on the parade ground in twenty minutes," Grierson said and left to do just that.

"Why not just have Grierson order them to go with us?" Harrison asked after Grierson left.

"A lot of men are going to die if we can find Quanah. The troops don't know me or you and may be reluctant to follow our orders even if ordered to by Grierson. I had rather let them see us beforehand. Listen to what we have to say and let them make up their mind whether they want to volunteer for a dangerous mission. I had rather have fifty men who will do as we say than a hundred who some may or may not accept us in charge. Troopers for the most part are loyal to the officers they know.

Twenty-five minutes later Tye and Harrison stood in front of over three hundred troops. Grierson addresses the troops and introduces Lieutenant Harrison and then Tye. At Tye's name a low mumbled roar came from the crowd as they all had heard of him. Grierson raised his arms, and it drew quiet quickly. Tye stepped forward to give his version of what he wanted.

"Two weeks ago, Lieutenant Harrison and myself along with a small troop of soldiers from Fort Clark ambushed Quanah Parker and about eighty of his warriors. After a thirty minute or so battle he withdrew his warriors and the Lieutenant and myself met him on the battlefield under a flag of truce. He was furious and embarrassed he had been outsmarted by the bluecoats. He swore he would be back with five hundred warriors and kill every man, woman and child at the fort. I led a small patrol up this way to see if he actually was going to do this. He is and has about four hundred warriors or so with him. If he continues his current path he will bypass Concho, but he will kill every white man and woman and child between here and Fort Clark to get his revenge."

"It was your Post Commander Grierson who suggested we meet him up here and try to prevent the massacre of men and their families that he would encounter on the way to Clark. I am telling you this because men will die in the effort, and I want men who will follow Lieutenant Harrison and my orders. I do not want men who are ordered to follow us but I want volunteers, men who believe they are doing the right thing to try and save innocent lives."

Before he could say anything else a large, bearded Sergeant stood up. "I volunteer Tye and asking the men who want to go join me over there toward the mess hall." He then walked away from the men. No one moved for a moment and Tye thought his idea of volunteers was dead then foolish then men started walking over to where the sergeant stood. They left in twos then in groups of five or six and then ten at a time. Tye was shocked when more than two hundred men volunteered. They were made up both Calvary and infantry, both white and the colored "Buffalo Soldiers".

Tye walked over to the Sergeant and introduced himself. "Tye Watkins he said offering his hand. First Sergeant Russel King took his hand in a firm handshake. "It's a pleasure to meet you Tye after all the stories we have heard about you."

"Don't believe everything you hear Sergeant and introduced Lieutenant Harrison who whispered.

"They are true, "Harrison whispered in King's ear.

"You know the men Sergeant?" Tye asked.

" I know the soldiers and the shirkers."

"Good. Pick me out one hundred of the Calvary troopers you know you can count on. No infantry as we will be moving fast."

"Yes Sir. Right away."

Tye and Harrison watched as King walked among the men separating them till he had one hundred. At that time Commander Grierson walked up to them.

"I see you have First Sergeant King picking your men."

"Is that a good thing?" Tye asked, "Or a bad thing."

Grierson laughed and answered. "It's a good thing. King is a top soldier. Been soldering for almost twenty years but don't let that fact make you think he is too old. There's not two men in this fort that could together, handle him in a fight. If he had an education he might be a general by now, but he is happy where he is and is my right hand." He looked over Tye's shoulder and spoke. "Here he comes now." Tye and Harrison both turned to see King coming.

King saluted Grierson and Harrison who both returned in kind. "Men are assembled Tye."

Tye walked among the men and knew Grierson knew what he was talking about. *These are top soldiers. Not your youngsters but solid, older veterans. These men will do*, he thought to himself. "You done well Sergeant. I'm impressed."

"They will follow you to hell if need be. Not a man among them that has not heard of you."

Tye stood before the men. Lieutenant Harrison and I along with First Sergeant King will lead you men against the finest fighting men you will ever face led by their greatest warrior Quanah Parker. There are one hundred of you and along with my twenty we will send their asses back north to their home with the tails between their legs. From looking at each of you I know we are equal to three or four of them to one of you." There was a tremendous yelling from the troops but even over noise Tye heard some rebel yells.

He held ups his hands and the noise subsided. Tye said. "I thought I heard some rebel yells amongst all the yelling. Who among you fought for the South?" No one said anything. "I'm not holding that against you. I would like to know who you are because I have yet to meet one of you rebels that were not hell on wheels in a fight." Seven men stood up. "Thank you Boys. Look forward to going into battle with you and going into battle it will be. We will muster here in two hours. Your Post Commander has ordered the ordinance man to issue thirty rounds each for your carbines and full belt for your side arms. Five-day rations will be available at the commissary. Get your things in order and I will see you in two hours."

In just a little under two hours the troops were on the move. Tye was impressed with the ordnance and the quartermaster with the speed they had things ready. A mile out of Concho Tye halted the column. He spoke with Lieutenant Harrison, First Sergeant King and his friend scout Dan August.

"Dan and me are going to scout east and north. We will find you later after you make camp."

"How will you find our camp?" King asked.

You only have about three hours riding before it is dusk. I can judge how far you will travel if you keep moving northeast. We will find you. Put your guards as usual but double them on the horses." King nodded and Tye and Dan rode away.

At dusk they came across a great number of unshod pony tracks. Kneeling while Dan kept watch, Tye studied the tracks. "Less than an hour old," Tye said.

"What are you thinking?"

"That we need to find their camp and make plans to attack it early in the morning." Tye answered. Two hours later, after full dark, they found the camp. Many fires burned.

"Most warriors I have ever saw," Dan whispered. "Must be close to five hundred or so."

"Damn sure enough to go around," Tye said. "Too many to ride through their camp. Would take too long and too many soldiers would die." He thought for a moment. "I have a better plan. We will use their old of luring them into a trap. Let's get back to our horses and go find our camp. They rode a mile west before heading south to avoid detection to find King and the camp.

It was almost midnight when they rode into camp after being stopped twice by guards which pleased both men. At least the camp was guarded well. King was waiting by a very small fire with rocks placed around it.

"Was afraid you got lost." He chuckled. "Here, have some coffee, hardtack and biscuits waiting for you." They all squatted around the fire. Did you find them?"

"Yes we did and there's a hell of lot of them," Dan said.

"I was going to attack their camp like we did a couple weeks ago," Tye said. We rode in and surprised them early in the morning before daylight. Caught them completely by surprise. We killed a few riding through and then stampeding their pony heard. But that camp wasn't large, and we were through it in less than twenty seconds. It would take much longer to ride through this one and I'm afraid we would lose a lot of men because even surprised they would get organized and fighting back quickly." He took a couple swallows of coffee. "This is what I think we need to do. We can use one of their tricks by luring them into a trap." He said we will take a few men, twelve or so like it is a patrol and let them be seen. The patrol in turn will turn tail and head south where we will be waiting for them. Hopefully in their wanting to kill bluecoats so bad they will chase them. We will find a place in their direction of travel that will provide us an opportunity to surprise them."

Quanah was upset. They had come across a homestead late yesterday and killed the man right off. Some of his warriors took pleasure in the wife and two daughters before killing and scalping them as well as the man. The cause of his unrest was the two hours they spent at the homestead. It had been late before all the celebrating was done so they spent the night there. He was anxious to get the Fort Clark and kill all of white eyes, especially Watkins. He spit on the ground at the mention of his name. They had been moving since first light this morning but as far as he was concerned were behind when he figured to be at Clark.

Tye had Sergeant Arnold pick a man who was sure could find his way back to Fort Clark with a dispatch from Lieutenant Harrison.

Major Thurston

Post Commander

Fort Clark, Texas

Have made contact with Quanah east of Fort Concho. Five hundred or so warriors.

We have one hundred troops from Concho. Tye is going to try and trap them and kill enough of them they will head back north. At worse we can delay them on their way to you. Three days away at least. Tye asks you to prepare for the worse

Your obedient servant

Lt. Harrison

Sergeant King sent a similar dispatch with a trooper to Fort Concho and Colonel Grierson. Tye had Dan, Harrison, and First Sergeant King gathered around him.

I'm going to scout north and try to find exactly what trail they are taking. I'm betting it will be southwest, a direct line to Clark, but I want to be sure. We will have only one chance at stopping him. Sergeant, you are familiar with the lay of the land around here. Is there any places we might lure them to?"

King answered. "A little farther south of where we are there are some hills and a couple rivers that have cut through the land."

"Take the men that way Sergeant King. Dan, you and Sergeant Arnold find a place suitable, then Dan, you take twelve men and ride north to find me. Once I have figured out their route I will ride south, find a hill and used my mirror to signal you where I am, and we can reunite. Dan can lead us toward the spot you have picked, and we will lead the

Comanche that way." Tye turned to Lieutenant Harrison. "Sir, you and King make arrangements for the ambush. If it was me, I would put thirty men on each side, twenty-five to close in behind and the men with Dan and me can turn and block their escape. I'm betting that Quanah when he sees the trap will turn his men to the right or left and charge that way up the hill."

"The men on the side he charges toward have no chance," Harrison said then added, "It will be a slaughter, thirty against four or so hundred."

"There's that chance Lieutenant but I don't think so. Sure we are going to lose men, maybe even you or me, but have your men in a tight bunch on the side of the hill and in two rows. Have the men fire alternately, first row then second row. They should get off at least two shots each then before the Comanche figure out what is going on and turn to escape. Use the Colts then. Thirty men using the six shot Colts is a lot of fire power. I'm betting the Comanche will break right and left and not over the troops."

"Thar's a lot of betting," King said smiling.

"Life is a gamble," Dan said. "When a soldier signs up, or a scout for that matter, he knows the danger and by signing accepts it." They all nodded their agreement.

Tye left to find the Comanche. The troops moved southeast to find an ambush site. With Sargent King and Harrison up front. King turned in the saddle to look up at the guidon flag of the troop's colors that the flag bearer held. It always filled him with pride seeing it snapping in the breeze. He turned to Harrison asked him how well he knew Tye.

"Only been with him once Sargent but the man lived up to his reputation at that time. We were fixing to be overrun by the Comanche and he jumped up screaming and charged the hostiles swinging his knife in one hand and his tomahawk with the other. He cut them down like a lumber jack does trees. The Comanche retreated. Sergeant Arnold said "*damn Tye you must be getting old. I only counted seven dead Comanche that you killed.*" "If you really want to know about Tye, ask Sargent Arnold back there because he has been on countless patrols with him." He turned in the saddle and hollered, "Sargent Arnold."

Arnold lightly kicked his horse forward and rode up alongside of Harrison. "Yes Sir."

"Sargent, Sargent King has a question for you. He wants to know about Tye and if the stories about some of the things he has done are true or exaggerated."

"Well Sargent, I don't know what you have heard but I'm sure it's probably understated. Tye is the only thing on earth the Apache are afraid of. So much that they had what we would call a bounty on him. No one collected and there were many who tried. He thinks like an Indian, he tracks like an Indian and reads sign probably better than an Indian. He is skilled not only with a rifle and pistol but with any kind of weapons and if he doesn't have any he will beat you to death with his fist. There's no one like him anywhere in this country and I'm damned proud to know him. He can go into a camp after you have left and within fifteen minutes tell you how many men you had, what you had for breakfast, and what direction you left in and then tell you if you had any horses limping and if you had pack animals. He thought for a minute and said. We were trapped by the Apaches one time because a stupid officer", he looked at Lieutenant Harrison, "Sorry Sir," then added, "That would not listen to Tye. We were trapped and could not get to our horses. He snuck out after dark and ran almost forty miles to the fort and brought back a troop to pull us out the next day about noon."

"That is one I had heard but did not believe it," King said.

"Well, you can now. Worse day of my life. The damn Apaches were above us on a cliff and all night long kept us awake by throwing rattlesnakes down on us every once in a while. We was in a pickle and none of us thought we would live through tomorrow even though we knew Tye had gone for help. Who would have thought that man could run almost forty miles to the fort? But my God he did and even though exhausted he mounted a horse and led the troops back to us. We had fought all morning but when the troops arrived we was fixing to get over run. I'll never doubt anything he says and nothing he does surprises me anymore. Every blasted trooper at Clark has had his butt saved more than once. If you ever catch him with his shirt off your eyes will open wide and you will stare with your mouth open at the site. His build is God given. There is no way one man should have the muscles he has. But that's only one thing. When you get past his muscles you will notice his scars: bullet holes, arrow holes, and knife wounds." Arnold chuckled and added, "The surgeon at the fort says he will never die because he has no vital organs."

After a few minutes Sargent King said. "That is the most amazing story I ever heard."

"Ain't no story Sargent. It's the God's truth. I could tell you a dozen more that I have seen him do the last few years that is hard to believe. I would doubt them myself if I had not witnessed them my own self. You may see for yourself in the next couple days if he brings the Comanche to us."

King said. "I'm sorter torn as to where I want him to bring them to us but then I think of all those folks between here and Clark and especially those at Clark."

"It's up to us King to make sure that don't happen," Harrison said. King nodded.

A few miles north Tye had an eye on a Comanche scout but could not see the main body and Quanah. As he watched from the top the low hill where he lay the scout passed by two hundred yards below him. Tye prayed he would keep going on the line he was traveling and not spot his horse tethered in some brush behind the hill he was on. A few anxious moments later the scout passed on by. Tye followed him staying to the right of his path and not ever taking a chance on being spotted by using the hills.

Tye rode a half mile farther to the right of the scout's path then turned south a nudged Sandy to a gallop to get ahead of the Comanche. Fifteen minutes later he figured he was far enough ahead and tuned Sandy left and trotted to where he hoped the scout would show up. He lay on top of a low hill hidden in the tall grass with his binoculars. Twenty minutes and no sign of the scout he thought he had guessed the wrong path. If he had, his plan of stopping Quanah would be in jeopardy. He decided to wait another fifteen minutes or so but first he turned around and checked behind him sweeping the area with his glasses to make sure he would not be surprised by the scout coming up behind him. He saw nothing but some antelope calmly grazing so he was sure no one was coming.

He turned back around and immediately saw the horse and rider about a quarter of a mile away. He put his left hand over the top of the binoculars to shade the sun and giving no chance of reflection. He saw the scout clearly now. He backed down the hill and mounted Sandy and walked to the west for a few minutes before turning him South again at a gallop. He rode for two or so miles before topping a hill that was pretty high and he had a good few of the land around him. Taking a mirror from one of his saddle bags he flashed it south a few times then watched. Ten minutes later he saw the patrol. Using his glasses, he saw Dan in the lead. He put the glasses and mirror back in the saddlebag and lightly nudged Sandy with his heels into a gallop and headed toward them.

Dan held up his hand to halt the patrol when he saw Tye coming toward them. Arriving Tye reached out to shake Dan's hand.

"Glad to see you Tye. We saw you flashing the mirror and I was glad to see it. I was afraid we had missed each other."

"Me too Dan but we don't have much time. There is a scout coming no more than a mile or two behind me. We need to make a temporary camp so the scout will see us and rush back to Quanah and the rest of the Comanche. They will come to kill us so once we are spotted we will mount our horses and wait for them. They made what looked like a camp but wasn't. Tye had instructed them not to be looking north as he wanted the scout to think he was unseen. Tye walked fifty or so yards away and lay down in the grass to watch. Fifteen minutes later he spotted the scout. As he watched through the binoculars the scout halted a little less than a quarter mile away and quickly reversed his direction and rode quickly away. Tye trotted back to the temporary camp and told the men they had been spotted.

"We will wait about ten minutes then mount up a slowly walk our mounts toward the Comanche. When they see us we will do an about face and lead them to the ambush."

A few minutes later as they walked their horses north they heard them before they spotted the first of the Comanche coming from around a low hill. The sheer sight of so many Indians was frightening enough but the fact they were so close, maybe three hundred yards. The patrol reversed their direction and headed at a fast gallop following Tye. Tye did not want any of their mounts to falter before they reached the other troops and if need be, could run all out when the Comanche mounts would be tiring out. Dan told him they were no more than three miles from the other troops.

Tye, riding beside Dan hollered out to him. "Go ahead and lead the men. I'm gonna fall back to the rear with the men to keep them from panicking." A few seconds later Tye was the last man in the detail. He looked over his shoulder at the charging warriors and realized they had closed to a little over one hundred yards. He knew their ponies could not run full out much longer. He decided to stop and incite them more. He whirled Sandy around and with his Henry rifle fired four quick shots. Two ponies were now rider less and the warriors after their riders were knocked backwards over the horse's rear and were trampled by the rushing horde behind them. Tye quickly reined Sandy around kicked him into an all-out run to catch up with the patrol. The lead warrior was fifty yards behind the patrol when all hell broke loose from the right and left of the patrol.

Dan halted the patrol and they spread out in a skirmish line and dismounting had their mounts lay down as they were trained to do. The troopers lay behind their mounts and fired their Spencer rifles and then pulled their Colt sidearm and lay down a devastating fire emptying several Comanche ponies who were milling around in the dust and smoke from the soldiers guns not really knowing which direction to go. The troopers were all around them and their brothers were being knocked off their ponies by the soldier's rifles. Suddenly they were headed back north where the twenty troopers were blocking their escape. As Tye predicted they were more interested in escaping the trap than killing bluecoats at this moment. They split and ran past the troopers on both sides. Some fired arrows as they rode past.

The soldiers stood and cheered waving their hats. Tye instructed the men with him to make sure there were no warriors left alive to kill an unsuspecting soldier. A few minutes later they had gathered their dead and wounded. They lost four men on the rear guard and one man with Tye. There were several wounded with arrows but none that would die from them. They counted forty-one Comanche dead and Tye was sure there was several more wounded. Tye would stay busy for two or so hours removing arrows and showing others how to.

Two miles north Quanah gathered his warriors. Little bear rode up to him.

"Little Bear saw the big scout from Fort Clark that ambushed us several moons ago."

"Two Bears saw him also," Two Bears said.

"Let us council," Quanah said. Quanah, Two Bears, Little bear, and Little Wolf sat in a circle with the other warriors a way off watching.

"Little Bear asked, his voice wavering not from fear but from anger, "Let us make the bluecoats pay for the killing of our brothers."

Two Bears spoke. "We will but let us be careful not to fall into a trap again."

"This scout Watkins is smart and thinks like an Indian as I have heard." Quanah said. "Twice now he has trapped us. Two Bears is right, we must be careful and not plunge into another trap and lose more of our brothers. This is what we will do. I know the bluecoats. They will take time to wrap their dead in blanket and care for their wounded, so they are probably still at the same place. Two Bears, take half of our warriors and ride around and come in behind the soldiers. Little Bear and myself will lead the rest and charge the soldiers from this direction and trap them in between us and kill them all."

Tye finished working on the last wounded man and walked over to where Lieutenant Harrison, and Sergeants Arnold and King were drinking coffee. King offered him a cup.

"Thanks Sargent."

"I'd say we kicked their Butts wouldn't you Tye, Harrison said smiling.

"We killed some but we are not out of the woods yet," Tye said.

156

"What do you mean Tye?" King asked. "They are probably still running north back to where they come from."

"I would like to think that Sargent but I don't think so."

"What do you mean by that Tye?" Harrison said his face no longer smiling.

"Quanah is mad like I said before. He is going to hit us again pretty quick with all he's got. He has to wipe us out to save face."

"What do you have in mind Tye?" Arnold asked.

"Have the men dig in here with twenty-five men facing north and twenty-five facing south. Have fifteen of your best shots on each slope is to our right and left. Over yonder," he said pointing with his rifle, "is a large cut in the hill with an arroyo that is deep enough to hold most of our horses, maybe all of them if we squeeze them close together. Have the remaining men protecting them."

"How long do you think we have?" Harrison questioned.

"Not long enough so we had better get busy. If he comes, I had rather fight him here than on the open prairie.

Arnold you take the men on the right slope and King you on the left. Tell your men to hold their fire till I fire. Understood?" Both men nodded their understanding. Five minutes later the men on the slopes and on the canyon floor were digging with their hands and knives in the soft earth to make room for them to lie down hoping the hole would protect them.

Twenty minutes later Sargent Arnold from his elevated position on the hill shouted, **"Here they come!"**

Tye muttered to himself but loud enough that Harrison heard, "Damn. This is one time I wish I had been wrong. He shouted, **"Get ready men and don't fire until I do."**

They all heard the pounding of the hooves. Four hundred horses, sixteen hundred hooves pounding the earth make a tremendous noise. A few seconds later they heard the sound coming from the Comanche warriors screaming their war cries.

Sargent King on the opposite side from Arnold screamed, **"They are coming from behind us."**

Tye looked over his shoulder and then hollered. **Arnold, King, have halve of your men turn their guns**

behind us." Tye turned back to face the ones coming in from the front and then turning an eye to those coming from the rear and then back to the front trying to gauge when to open fire.

The troopers to a man wanted to open up but fear of Tye made them wait. Sweat poured from faces and the men continually wiped the sweat from their hands. Wait! Wait! Each man told himself. At one hundred yards they waited. Finally, Tye opened up with his repeating Henry rifle.

Almost one hundred rifles opened up as one and the result was predictable-a great number of ponies with no riders continued the charge. Tye fired his rifle till it clicked on an empty chamber with only a few bullets not finding flesh. The charge did not break but continued toward them. Most of the troopers, their hands trembling, were not able to reload their rifles and fumbled at getting their side arms out. The Comanche swerved at the last instant in both front and the rear and charged up the slopes toward King and Arnold. They swept past them shooting arrows. Even as proficient as a Comanche warrior is with a bow, it's difficult to hit a target with you pony racing up a hill and the enemy shooting at you. In a few seconds they were over the hill and racing back to the front of the small canyon to regroup.

Lieutenant Harrison stood and hollered at King and Arnold." I need a casualty report. He looked at the men with Tye and himself and counted eight dead and eleven wounded.

Sargent King sounded off." Four dead and four wounded."

Sargent Arnold shouted. "Five dead and six wounded."

"Damn," Harrison muttered, "seventeen dead and twenty-one wounded."

Tye hollered. "Arnold, you and king come on down and bring the dead and wounded." After they arrived Tye quickly had a couple men he had worked with yesterday with the wounded helping him now. "Get the arrows out a quickly as possible and bandage them up as quickly as possible and if possible get them in position to fight again." He turned to King, Arnold and Harrison. "They will hit us again and I believe they will all come from the front intending to overrun us in one charge. Have the men in three rows of equal number or as closes as you can to equal. Front row will fire and then reload as the second-row fires and then the third. The first row should be able to fire again but the second and third need to pull their Colts." Tye stood up after the men were assembled in the rows. "Men, we all just withstood an attack by over four hundred warriors. I would like to commend each of you for standing your ground. Look around you and look at the dead Comanche. There is a lot of them. They are fixing to hit us again but not with near as many warriors. We fought them off once and we can do it again. It may get nasty, hand to hand fighting. But it's like I have told the men at Clark, when it gets nasty and things look bad that is when you have to get mean, I mean be as mean as a damn she-bear protecting her cubs. Scream louder than the Comanche, be as hard to kill as a Comanche and fight dirtier than them. If you can do this we just may show the Comanche just what a soldier and fighter we are." At this last word a tremendous yell erupted from the troops.

"Hell of a speech Tye," Harrison said smiling, then asked. "Do you really think we can hold them off?"

"Hell yes Lieutenant. I intend to see my wife and kids again. If every man goes kind of crazy mad if it comes to hand to hand, we have a chance."

"You mean like you do Tye." Arnold said smiling.

Tye shrugged and said, "Maybe I do sometimes." Tye shrugged, "Maybe I do every once in a while," he said smiling. "This attack coming will be a little different, so I want you to know ahead."

"In what way?" King asked.

"We hurt them pretty bad," Tye answered. "They are pissed and if I know anything about Indians, they will be coming and will not stop this time. They will come in one wave with the intention of over running us and killing all of us in the process, so we need to get ready. King you take twenty men and get on the left slope and Arnold take twenty and set up on the right. Have your men dig in and pile the dirt high in front. Lieutenant, can you get the men together before we spread out?"

"Arnold. You and King get the men here," Harrison ordered.

With the men all around him Tye spoke. "Each of you did well a while ago. I'm here to tell you that it's not over in fact the worse is yet to come. They will be coming shortly so I am telling you what to expect. The Comanche will come in one large force with one intention, over running our position and killing every last one… everyone. It's going to get nasty hand to hand with knives and rifle butts. To survive you are going to have to get nasty yourself, go crazy mean. **Can you do this?**" He screamed. There was a quietness among the group then slowly the hollering and screaming came forth from every man.

"King, you and Arnold get your men on the slopes," Lieutenant Harrison said. You have the remaining men get in two rows here with Tye and me. We will fire alternately, row one, then row two and then one again. Get to it." The men did as ordered, about thirty in first row and twenty five in second row. "The wounded will have to fight any way possible," he added. "Private Bailey, will you make sure the wounded are with a loaded Spencer and a loaded Colt?"

"Yes Sir, Lieutenant."

Fifteen minutes later the troopers once again felt the ground trembling and the noise of several hundred hooves striking the ground. A minute later they heard the screams of the Comanche. To a man they had hoped Tye was wrong, even Tye hoped he was, but he wasn't. Tye has been in countless fights with the Apache and even some with the Comanche but never a direct assault like this with four hundred or so warriors. "STAND YOUR GROUND. DON'T LET YOUR BUDDY NEXT TO YOU DOWN," Tye screamed.

Guns exploded from the sides of the canyon and several warriors were on their way to the hereafter. Tye fired and the front line fired almost as one then the second row fired. By the time the first row fired again dust and smoke made accurate shooting almost impossible. The Comanche was upon them and leaping from their ponies' backs attacking the troopers with knives and war clubs. Tye had his hands full being in the center of the first row. He bashed one warrior's skull with his tomahawk and gutted another with his 10" Bowie. One could not see much in all the dust and smoke, both Comanche and troopers were attacking anything moving around them.

Arnold and King had the best rifleman, and they were sending hell and damnation down on the Comanche that were still mounted and milling around. The troopers on the hill were above the dust and could shoot accurately. After a few moments Quanah took control of his braves and sent several charging up both sides toward the men on the hill. A man next to King took an eight-foot spear in the chest that protruding three foot out his back. King was swinging his nine-pound Spencer like a war club and was being very effective with it. Another trooper close to him screamed as a Comanche drove his knife into his chest.

It was mayhem everywhere. Comanche war screams, gun fire, screams of the wounded and dying. Whenever he had the chance Tye could see soldiers fighting like mad men. A warrior jumped from his pony and hit Tye like a bull buffalo knocking him on his back but not stunning him which was good because immediately the Comanche was raising his knife to plunge into his chest. He blocked the knife with his left arm and received a deep cut. He immediately drove his Bowie to the hilt in the brave's chest and threw him off and stood up and split anther Indians skull with his tomahawk who was on Lieutenant Harrison's back. Harrison acknowledged the act and was immediately fighting with another warrior.

Arnold on the right slope had the same situation as King had. More than enough Comanche to go around. He was proud of his men as no one had broken and run and were fighting like hell. He had two in front of him trying to decapitate him. He dispatched one with the butt of his Spenser and ducked the roundhouse swing of the Comanche tomahawk on his right and came up with his knife with his right hand and ripped the warrior's belly open spilling blood and guts out on his hand and the ground.

Dan August was close To Tye and Harrison when he saw something that made him almost laugh and thought *I wondered when it was going to happen.* Tye had jumped out of the hole and standing on the dirt from the hole started screaming and could be heard over everything else. Dan never knew how he could scream that loud and knew what was coming. Tye, still screaming, began walking down the row of raised dirt swinging his tomahawk in his left hand and slicing and stabbing with his Bowie in his right. Several startled Comanche died in the next few seconds. The troopers not engaged watch in awe at the scene. Arnold and some of the troopers from Clark stayed busy with the Comanche. They had witnessed it before.

All of a sudden a Warrior on a black pony released an arrow that struck Tye in the left upper chest, almost in his shoulder. Tye went down. You could almost feel the despair from the troopers who saw this, but elation came immediately afterwards as Tye stood up and broke the shaft with his right hand and threw it at the Comanche and immediately let loose with his impersonation of a rebel yell, swinging his Bowie with his right hand and holding his bleeding left from the earlier knife cut across his chest and killing Comanche again. A that time he did not know Quanah had put the arrow in him and what resulted with his throwing it unknowingly at Quanah.

Quanah, who had released the arrow, was astonished the scout rose and continued to fight, even breaking the arrow shaft and throwing it at him. The Great War Chief had seen enough and called his warriors to him and away from the bluecoats and the crazy scout.

Tye looked around as did all the other troopers that were standing and not believing the Comanche pulled out of the fight. On the floor of the canyon and on both sides were dead Comanche and soldiers. Many of the soldiers standing were wounded and some unable to stand. Harrison, bleeding from the side of his head dispatched soldiers to finish off any wounded Comanche.

Tye sat down weak from is wounds. Every soldier that could came by and shook his hand knowing he had inspired them to this victory. Arnold had a slight head wound and had wrapped his bandana around his head. He was speaking with King and Harrison.

Arnold said. "Glad the both of you got out of this in one piece." Both men had slight wounds but not very many of the men were without one or more.

King said. "Someday someone will write a book about that man over there. I haven't known him long, but I can write a chapter."

"Best part is coming," Arnold commented.

"What's that mean?" Harrison asked.

"He is fixing to get that arrow out and he will take his shirt off then you will see what I'm talking about."

Tye had one of the men who had been helping him with the wounded earlier going to remove the arrow. The three of them walked over to where Tye was. Tye looked up and spoke to Harrison.

"Do you have a casualty report yet?"

Harrison nodded. "Thirty-one dead and forty-two injured of which sixteen cannot ride but most should make it. We counted eighty-nine dead Comanche. Don't know how many were wounded."

"We hurt him bad Lieutenant. I think he will go back to the canyon where his main camp is. You can bet with the losses today and the number of wounded half of his force is done fighting at least for a while." He looked at the private who was waiting to remove the arrow. "Make sure all the wounded are cared for and then come back here." He turned to Sergeant Arnold. "Help me out of this shirt you old cuss." When the shirt was removed they all saw that there was a slight bulge on his back where the tip was but had not broken the skin. Those standing around then was amazed at what they saw all except Arnold. The build of this man was unbelievable. Then they saw the scars all over his torso.

Tye handed Arnold his knife. "You know what you need to do. Go to one of the fires and get this knife hot." By this time several troopers were gathered around. A few minutes later Arnold returned with the knife blade glowing red. He cut the skin where the point was. He moved to the front of Tye.

"You ready?" Tye nodded. Arnold cut the shaft in to about ten inches from Tye's chest. He picked up a flat rock. He told the private that had been helping Tye with the wounded. "When I knock the arrow threw you grab the shaft just above the tip and jerk it straight out and do it in one motion. He looked at Tye and he nodded. He slammed the rock on to the shaft and the private jerked it out. The whole process took about two seconds. Arnold then took the still glowing knife and sealed the wounds in front and back. Tye broke out in a sweat and other than a low grunt made no sound. Arnold removed the bandage from Tye's left arm to seal it, but it had quit bleeding.

Tye was hurting but chuckling to himself, "he had to live up to his image," so he stood up shrugged his massive shoulders, put his shirt on and saw his fellow scout and friend. He motioned to Dan to follow him. They walked away from all the men.

Dan said. "You want me to follow Comanche?" The two men had been friends for a long time, and it did not surprise Tye that his friend was reading his mind.

Tye smiled despite the pain in his shoulder and arm and answered. "I was going to but I'm not in condition to do it. Just follow them till you are sure they are not coming back." How many men are left from Clark that came with us?"

"Four that are not wounded, five dead. All the wounded can ride."

"Go ahead and scout. I'm taking all the men from Clark including the dead back to Clark. We will moving slow so find Sergeant King at Fort Concho and tell him what you saw. I will meet with him in a minute and make arrangements for a fresh horse and supplies for you and come on to meet us on the trail. Like I said we will be traveling slowly because of the wounded, including myself. Don't you take any chances you old cuss." Dan laughed at the statement about Tye wanting to travel slow.

"My God, you are human."

Tye walked back to the men and finding Harrison, Arnold, and King sat down and talked.

King asked. "Where is Dan going?"

"I think they are whipped and going back to their main camp, but one never knows what an Indian is thinking so I wanted Dan to follow them to make sure they are going back. He will report to you at Concho. If you can arrange for him a fresh horse and some grub so he can catch up with me. I'm taking the men back to Clark, all of them including our dead that is if it's okay with the lieutenant.

Lieutenant Harrison nodded, "Of course but are you in condition to ride?"

Tye nodded and walked off to where the dead were lying. Arnold followed.

Tye said. "Can you get five horses and have the men that came with us wrapped in a blanket with a ground cloth wrapped around the blanket to keep them dry if it rains, then get the rest ready to ride." Arnold nodded.

Arnold passed King and Harrison. King asked. "Don't you think Tye is hurting too much to ride the three days back to Clark?"

Arnold answered. "Hell yes he is but he is Tye Watkins and can't let the men see that he can be slowed down by a little old arrow and is actually human." He then added. "Hell man, he has a reputation to uphold," and laughed.

Dan caught up with Tye and the men a day out of Fort Clark with the news that the Comanche were headed to their main camp. Tye got him a fresh horse and told him to get to Clark and give Thurston the good news.

The next day the patrol with the wounded sitting with backs straight and chest out rode down the street of Brackett and into the Fort. Men, women, and kids lined the street in Brackett waving and shouting and when they entered the fort, soldiers lined the road up to post headquarters saluting them as they rode by. The best part for Tye was seeing Rebecca and the kids along with old Buff standing on the porch with Major Thurston. Lieutenant Harrison had the men line up in front of the porch and then gave the order to dismount. Some had to be helped from the saddle, but all stood at attention the best they could.

"At ease men," Thurston said forgoing protocol of passing the order through the chain of command. "I received the report of what you men did from Dan August. The fact that you did what you did being outnumbered five to one is the most remarkable feat I have ever heard of."

One of the men shouted "We had Tye with us sir. He wasn't going to let us lose." A chorus of shouts and calling Watkins name over and over from not only from the men who had fought but from those that had lined the road that had followed. Tye with the help of Thurston who came down the steps made his way up the porch and into the arms of Rebecca and the children. He turned to the men.

"I have never been prouder of anything in my life Major than leading these men into a battle where the odds were so insurmountable against them. Everyone did their job and never took a step back"

"Hell Tye, we were more afraid of you than the damn Comanche," another soldier yelled much to the delight of everyone. Even Thurston had to smile at the remark.

Tye held up his good arm and it got quiet. "Let us have a moment of silence for the five men that gave their lives. He then proceeded to call their names: Corporal Lance

Joiner, Private James Harper, Private Leslie Standridge, Private Billy Lester, and Private George O'Keefe."

Major Thurston said, "We will have services in the morning. Now, the staff at the post hospital are waiting on the wounded.

As the men dispersed Tye gave Rebecca a hug and kissed the kids. He stepped over to Buff and gave him a hug with his one good arm. He turned back to Rebecca and the kids. "I'll be along home soon as old sawbones gets through with me.

"Yu keep working fer the dang Armee sun, yu ain't gonna hav anee places left fer anee mo scars," Buff chuckled.

Authors note: Quanah continued to raid but the buffalo were almost gone which was their main source for food, shelter, and clothes. On June 2nd 1875 he surrendered at Fort Sill his people sick and starving. He is considered one of the greatest of the Comanche war chiefs. No one hated the white man more than he did but after surrendering he adopted to the white man's way of life. He became a spokesman for the Comanche and was

considered Chief of all the Comanche. He became friends with Teddy Roosevelt. He gave the ranchers permission, for so much a head, to drive their cattle across the reservation and divided the money up with all Comanche twice a year. The ranchers were so impressed that they built him a two-story house for him and his wives near the Wichita Mountains and was moved after his death in 1911 to Cache Oklahoma near Fort Sill. The main contributor to the house was Samuel Burnett owner of the 6666 Ranch. The house still stands and has a historical marker. He is buried in the Post Oak Mission Cemetery in Cache next to his white mother, Cynthia Ann Parker.

Gary McMillan

The Reynolds Gang

A short story

Chapter One

Frank Bingham, president of the First Bank of Uvalde, was leaving Bess's Restaurant where he had breakfast and coffee every morning of the week. It's five minutes to eight and if Frank was anything, he was known for his promptness. The bank opened at eight o'clock and he was always on time. He opened the door for his two male employees and two customers who were waiting. After acknowledging everyone he asked the two customers to be seated as it would take a minute to get things ready for business.

Across the street two brothers, Isaac and Billy James, sat on a bench outside the Bess's Restaurant watching the bank. They were waiting for the lady who owned the saloon to come out and walk across the narrow dusty street to make her deposit from the weekend business. When she did Isaac stood up and walked to the end of the plank walkway and stepping down turned left in the alley to where the rest of the gang waited. This was the notorious Reynolds gang led by Isaac and Billy Reynolds. They have been robbing banks all over the State of Texas for the last two and half years and leaving no witnesses alive. All members of the gang had been identified over time but knowing someone and finding him is difficult in a state as large as Texas. Despite posters being sent out all over the state no one had come forth, probably from fear of reprisal from this vicious bunch.

Buck sent Jesse Reynolds and Buck James down the street west of the bank to cover their escape. The two walked their horses about a hundred yards from the bank and after tying their mounts reins loosely on the hitching post stood by watching. Isaac and Billy entered the bank while Rufus Jones stood across the street with the horses.

Inside the bank Buck announced this is a holdup. One of the customers. A local rancher turned and started to draw his Colt. Billy standing close to the rancher busted his head with the barrel of his Colt knocking the man cold. Isaac demanded the money in the drawers and vault which had been opened to get cash for the two clerks. The door stood open, and Isaac jumped the counter and went to the vault pulling cash from the shelves into a bag while Billy held his gun on the people in the Bank. He walked to the woman from the saloon to relieve her from the bag she was carrying. She slapped Billy viciously and Billy staggering back shot her in the chest. Then he shot the rancher he had cold cocked in the back as he lay of the floor.

"Got the money Billy," Isaac hollered as he leapt back over the counter. "Let's get the hell out of here before the town realizes what's happening." Getting to the door, both men turned and shot the other people in the store. Across the street a man wearing a badge came out of the restaurant waving his Colt. He received two bullets in the chest from Rufus at point blank range who was holding the horses in front of Bess's. The three men jumped in the saddles and headed west. Two men came out of the hardware store and were cut down by Jesse and Buck who then mounted their horses and raced to catch up with the rest of the gang.

Two miles out of town they split into three groups. Billy and Buck, Isaac and Jesse, and Rufus riding by himself. This was pre-planned to throw off or at least slow down any pursuit by a posse. They would meet up a mile south of the Old Mail Road on the Nueces River. The old Mail Road was the road they rode out of Uvalde which ran through Brackett and Fort Clark almost to the Rio Grande River then swung north where it goes to Fort Davis and then to El Paso ending up in San Diego California.

Later that, about dusk the men started showing up where Isaac and Jesse waited: first was Rufus and fifteen minutes later, Billy and Buck.

"Any trouble?" Isaac asked as Billy and Buck dismounted. Rufus had had no problems.

"Just one old bastard that stayed on our trail," Billy said. "He won't be trailing no one ever again. Looked like one of them trappers the way he was dressed, floppy hat and buckskins. Hell, he even carried one of them old flintlock rifles and a damn knife almost as big as a sword. I'll say this for him, he stayed on our trail like a damn Injun no matter how we tried to fool him."

"I take it he is dead? "Isaac said questionably.

"Deader than a piece of old driftwood," Buck said. "Shot him in the forehead. Half his head exploded out the back of his skull. Took this off'n him." He walked to his saddle bags and took the knife Billy was talking about out of his saddle bag.

"Damn," Rufus exclaimed. "Would you look at that?" He turned the knife over and over in his hand studying it. "Bet that old bastard took lot of scalps with this thing." He handed it back to Buck.

"We'll rest here for a while then make our way west toward Mexico thru Brackett. We'll camp in a couple hours. I want to put a little more distance between us and Uvalde," Isaac stated.

"How about telling what the take was?" Rufus asked.

"About fifteen thousand, give or take a little. Just made a quick count, Isaac said then added. "I figure with the other robberies we have a twenty-five thousand or so total which we will split five ways when we get to Mexico."

"Sound good to me," Rufus said. "But" he added, "We may have a problem."

What problem?" Isaac asked.

When I was riding in Mexico before I met you and Billy I heard of this scout at Fort Clark that even the Apaches feared."

"The Apaches feared him," Billy said spitting disgustingly a wad of tobacco. "Apaches fear no one.'"

"They feared him enough that they put out what we call a bounty on him. Lots of Apaches have tried to earn it but they are dead. A couple years ago, maybe three there was the Valdez brothers whose gang were raising hell along the border. They made the mistake of robbing an army payroll and killing the men guarding it execution style-you know lined them up on their knees and shot each one in the back of the head. Left them for the buzzards. They scalped them and stuck a couple arrows in a couple of them making it look like the Indians did it. This scout, Watkins I think it was, tracked them down and killed every one but the leader. He beat the hell out of him not once, but twice before they hung him."

"Do you think we should go to Fort Clark and just surrender? Isaac asked Rufus. Billy and Jesse were laughing.

"Hell no Isaac. I just wanted ya'll to know about him and we don't need to do anything in Brackett to raise attention that might get him on our trail."

"Well, I don't know about this man Watkins you talked about is true or fiction, but just in case, we will be careful in the town," Isaac said.

182

At Fort Clark Tye, Rebecca, Buff, and the kids along with Lieutenants Harrison and Bullis were gathered around a small fire roasting some venison that Tye had killed earlier that day. Master Sargent O'Malley and his wife along with Major Thurston_was also in attendance. The mood was festive with a lot of laughter and bantering back and forth with most of it at Tye directed at his many scars.

"I bet when Rebecca rubs his back it feels like a washboard," Lieutenant Bullis said laughing along with everyone else.

Well, it's not quite that bad," Rebecca said laughing, "But close to it." This brought another round of laughter.

And so, it went for the next two hours when the venison that was cooked was gone, the corn and potatoes gone and the three dozen donuts Rebeca made were eaten the women and children went inside and left the men to their "man talk."

Major Thurston lit a cigar and most of the others rolled themselves a smoke. "Not often we can all get together and relax and have some pleasant talk without needing to figure out what we are going to do about a certain problem," the major said. I wish Captain McClelland was here, but he is on patrol and Dan is scouting. Anyway, I want to thank each of you for your part in the Comanche problem, namely Quanah. He hasn't lost too many fights but has lost twice to us with the help of Fort Concho."

"That's what bothering me Major. We embarrassed him twice and I don't think he's going to forget it," Tye said.

"You really think he may come back?" Bullis asked.

"I sure as hell would, wouldn't you? He's lost some of the mystique about him and he is going to want to get it back. He's a breed Sir, and it won't take much to make the rest lose faith in him. I'm sure there are some who resented him before and are probably talking to the others. Yes, I think he will come back even if it's by himself to get his revenge one soldier or scout at a time."

Thurston chuckled. "Well, one thing is for sure, you gave us something to think about." He looked around and spoke. "I wasn't going to bring this us but since Tye sorter put a damper to things, I will. There is a gang of cut-throats that hit a bank in Uvalde yesterday and killed about seven or eight people including a deputy sheriff. They are reportedly headed west, probably Mexico but could come through Brackett. They are believed to be a gang led by two brothers,

Isaac and Billy Reynolds and are totally ruthless. They never leave anyone alive. I have posted men on the outskirts of town with orders not to confront them but report to me if they see anything suspicious." He looked at Tye. "You brought down the Vasquez gang and the Yancey Cates gang of worthless pieces of dung plus all the men you brought down as a U.S. Marshall so your help may be needed again."

"Nothing else going on so I guess I'm available," Tye replied.

The rest of the evening was more smoke, more drinks, and a lot of war stories."

At five AM there was a knock of Tye's door.

"Who could that be at this time of the morning?" Rebecca asked.

"Not sure," Tye said pulling on his pants, "But it can't be good news."

A private was at the door and said Major Thurston asked you to come to his office right away.

"Let me finish dressing and I'll be there," Tye said and walked back to the bedroom to finish dressing.

"What is it, darling?" Rebecca asked.

"Don't have a clue, Honey. I'll be back as soon as I can."

Arriving at headquarters Tye was met by an orderly and ushered into Thurston's office where he found Captain McClellan, Lieutenants Harrison and Bullis along with Master Sargent O'Malley.

Tye shook everyone hand and while shaking McClelland's hand said, "I thought you were on patrol Captain."

"I was Tye," McClelland answered," But had to get back with some news."

"Which brings us to why we are all here this time of the morning," Thurston said. "Five men rode into Brackett about two o'clock his morning. They rode horses that were a lot better stock than the average cowboy rides and wore their guns tied down. They rousted the owner of the stables out and had him stable and feed their mounts then they went to the Sargent Hotel and got two rooms after banging on the doors to get someone to give them a room. I'm thinking they may be the bank robbers that hit Uvalde, so I have eight men outside the hotel to greet them when they walk out."

"The second thing is a report that McClelland brought to me. He ran into a patrol forty or so miles south of here from Fort Duncan. They had been pretty well shot up with several dead and wounded men. They had been ambushed by about a hundred or so Apaches. After a day long battle and standoff, the Apaches head north along the Rio Grande River. The lieutenant thought it was Juh leading them. I think…" he was cut off by a tremendous amount of gunfire from town.

They all jumped up and headed out of headquarters and ran toward Los Moras Creek Bridge that led into the town. As they crossed the bridge they saw five riders headed west with one apparently wounded. Tye and the others headed toward the hotel. There, they found the soldiers, five dead and three wounded. One of the wounded was leaning against the hitching post.

"What happened soldier?" Thurston asked.

"The men came out of the hotel, and we had them dead to rights. They raised their hands like they were surrendering, and I guess we sorter relaxed. Then when Riley over there went to get their guns they all dropped their hands and drew their guns so fast it was unbelievable. First thing I know I am shot in the shoulder and on the ground.

They were firing as fast as they could pull the triggers on their guns. I rolled over on my stomach and got off a shot and I think I hit one of them." The outlaws ran the short distance to the stables and got their horses saddled quickly, shot the stable owner and rode west out of town. They had helped the injured man, Jesse, on to his saddle and told him to hold on to the saddle horn. Billy had Jesse's horse's reins.

"You did soldier," Tye said. "We saw them riding off and one was laying low in the saddle like he was trying to stay in the saddle."

"You want me to go get them Major? Dan can scout for any patrol you are sending to find the Apaches."

Thurston nodded. "Pick five men to go with you. Give Sargent O'Malley their names and they will be brought to headquarters by the time you gather your things."

Tye left knowing that whoever is leading the troops to find Juh would be in good hands with Dan scouting for them. He had given the names to O'Malley who left to get the men he wanted. The men, First Sargent Arnold, Corporal Gary Garner, Pvt. Dickie Bailey, Pvt James Riley, Pvt. Dan Williams, and Pvt. George Reardon. Of the men, Arnold was well known to Tye and was a friend who could be counted on when things got out of hand. He had seen the other four

188

men in the fight with the Comanche and thought they would handle themselves well again.

When Tye got to his home he found everything he needed on the porch with Rebecca and Buff sitting on the steps waiting on him.

"How in the world did you know I would be leaving?" Tye asked Rebecca.

Rebecca smiled and answered him. "Been married to you long enough that when you are required to see Major Thurston immediately you are going to be leaving immediately. You going after the outlaws or the Apaches?"

Tye took her hand and helped her up off the step and hugged her. "The outlaws, but how did you know?"

"I told her Tye," Buff said. "She asked me whut us men talked abut last nite an I told her."

Tye nodded. "Hopefully I won't be gone long, maybe two- or three-days Honey." He kissed her and said Sargent Arnold and the men would be waiting on him. "Hug the kids", who were still asleep, "For me."

Chapter Two

The men were waiting when Tye got back to headquarters and were now on their way out of town after Major Thurston wishing them good luck. Captain McClellan along with Lieutenant Bullis and newly appointed Sargent Dickie Bailey were leaving a little later looking for Juh and his band of Warriors.

As they left the western edge of Brackett Tye had Arnold and Bailey ride on each side of the road looking for tracks leaving the road. This looking for tracks was slow going. The road bed and the ground on either side was dry and the slight breeze was blowing the sand and it was possible if one was not looking close to miss them. Ten miles out Bailey pulled up and hollered at Tye.

"Some tracks over here Tye. Looks to be three or four sets." Tye rode over, dismounted and studied the tracks.

"Five horses and made within last two or three hours," Tye mumbled. Let's take a chance these are theirs. He mounted Sandy and they headed southwest off the Old Mail Road. The ground was a little harder away from the road making tracking easier. Tye noticed one of the horses left hind leg turned in slightly and it looks like another had a slight limp probably from a stone bruise or a loose shoe."

Bailey was watching and listening but could not tell any difference in the tracks. He shook his head and thought, *Got myself a hell of lot to learn.* Bailey was married and lived in the enlisted men's barracks until he received his promotion from Major Thurston thanks to Tye's recommendation. Bailey brought his wife, Kay, to the fort from their home in San Antonio. She was a tiny thing and pretty as a picture. They had been to Tye's home where Rebecca cooked a great meal and Kay and Rebecca become fast friends and saw each other almost daily from then on.

An hour after leaving the road Tye saw that they were on the right trail. Tye pointed out to Bailey where they had stopped and one of the men, the wounded one had sat and leaned up against a large boulder. Blood stains on the rock and the ground showed he was hit hard and would definitely slow them down. "These are the men we are after, so we had better stay sharp. Thurston said they have killed no telling how many people besides the soldiers and civilians in Brackett. They trailed them till almost dark and then made camp.

Tye made the fire small and puts rocks all around it to keep prying eyes from locating them by their glow of their fire. Coffee was made and placed on the fire. "We will put the fire out as soon as the coffee is hot." Most of the men soaked their hardtack in their coffee making it soft enough to chew and swallow. "Arnold, you make the guard duty list. I'll take the last watch. I will be back in an hour or two. I'm going to scout ahead on foot to look things over."

Five miles from where the soldiers camp the five outlaws had made camp. Jesse Goodson lay on his blanket in terrible pain. Buck said, "That bullet has to come out or Jesse's done for."

Billy Reynold said. "We all know that Buck but it's deep in his back, probably in his innards. Only a doctor could get it out without killing him and they ain't no doc around here. If he makes it to Mexico we will get him doctored proper. Just keep pouring rot gut on it and hope it don't get infected."

"Shit and double shit," Isaac shouted. "Of all the damn luck we had to walk out of that motel right into the damn soldiers. If what you said," looking at Rufus, "is true about that scout at Clark I guarantee he is on our trail right now." Everyone looked around and Buck stood up and walked to the edge of the glow of their fire so he could see outside the firelight.

Rufus said, "Mabee we had better put out the fire."

Isaac kicked dirt on the fire. "Rufus you take first watch. Buck will relieve you in two hours then Billy and I'll take the last one. Rufus, before you start your watch give Jesse the rest of that bottle of rot gut. May help him go to sleep."

A little farther south Juh was camped with his war party. He was still feeling good about his last victory over the patrol from Fort Duncan. He sat on a large boulder in the middle of camp and looked all around at his Apache brothers: Some sleeping others talking quietly among themselves. Every once in a while one of the braves would look up at Juh and nod. To a brave, they respected him both as a leader and as a fierce warrior with more than fifty notches on his coup stick representing the number of enemies he has touched.

"Can we speak," came a familiar voice from behind him. Juh turned to his friend, Nantan, and climbed down from the boulder only to find Nana and Kuruk with Nantan. These three were his best friends and most trusted of the warriors who rode with him.

"Something the matter?" Juh asked.

The three looked at each other and finally Nantan spoke.

"We were wondering what your plan is and where are we going? We are only one night's sleep from the fort called Clark where the big scout is."

"Are the three of you afraid of this scout?"

Nana spoke. "No, not afraid but why do we look for trouble when not need be. Plenty of Mexicans to kill."

"We are going to cross river into Mexico to kill Mexicans but if the scout gets in way, we kill him." That seemed to satisfy the three friends.

Two miles to the north, the thirty-man patrol from Clark was camped. Lieutenant Bullis sat on his blanket drinking coffee and talking to his scout Dan August and First Sargent Gregory.

"Does it bother you that we have not seen Juh and his bunch or even any tracks yet?" He asked Dan.

"Not really Lieutenant. If you had been out here as long as me and Sargent Gregory have you would know the only time you see an Apache is when he wants you to see him. I'm thinking he is going along the river and going to cross into Mexico to kill Mexicans which the Apache hate more than the white soldiers. I think we will cross his tracks tomorrow if we head due west to the Border."

"I agree with Dan Lieutenant," Gregory said. "Lord knows they have reason to hate the Mexicans."

"Why is that?"

Gregory continued. "Years ago, the Mexican government put a bounty out for Apache scalps, and it made no difference if it was a warriors, squaw, or child. More than one friendly Apache was killed for that reason. Hell, the scalp hunters even killed Mexicans and sold their scalps since it was hard to tell the difference."

They hit their blankets early with the plan to head for the Border in the morning.

Sometime during the night Jesse died. The others lay him a shallow grave and put rocks on top to keep the varmints from digging him up. Rufus asked.

"Can we say some word over him?"

"You can if you feel there's a need but I for one am getting the hell to Mexico," Isaac said, and jumped on to his saddle and kneed his horse west follow by Billy and Buck.

Rufus watched them for a couple of seconds the mounted his horse and looking down at where Jesse was laid to rest said. "He done some bad thinks Lord, but he told me he was a beliver so have mercy on him. Amen." He kneed his horses and followed the others.

Tye and his group were on their way the next morning as soon as it was light enough to follow the tracks of the outlaws. An hour later he halted the group and sniffed the air. There's a campfire close by. Ya'll wait here while I take a looksee."

Lieutenant Harrison sniffed the air but smelled nothing. He turned to Arnold. "You smell anything?"

"No, but if Tye says there is a campfire close by, you can bet there is." A few minutes later they saw Tye motioning them to come on. Arriving where Tye was Tye said.

"We missed them by no more than an hour. The wounded man died and is buried there," he pointed with his rifle. They saw the mound of rocks and the campfire that was still smoking. Arnold looked at Harrison just as the lieutenant looked at him. Harrison shook his head and Arnold just smiled.

Noticing this, Tye asked. "What the hell is funny Arnold?"

Lieutenant Harrison spoke. "We could not smell any smoke, but Arnold told me that if you said there's a campfire, there will be a campfire."

Tye smiled. "That's neither here or there. Just proves neither of you can smell worth a crap," he said laughing. "Seriously though," he said, "We are close, and they probably suspect we or someone from Bracket is following them so we had better be on our toes and be ready for anything, especially an ambush. This bunch is ruthless and four or five more dead soldiers is nothing to them."

"What do we do then?" Harrison asked.

"I can tell you Lieutenant," Arnold said. "Tye is good at sniffing out trouble so it's up to me and you to keep ourselves and the men ready for trouble in an instant."

"That pretty well sums it up," Tye said. "I'm going to be a quarter mile or so in front. If you hear gun shots come running but come carefully at the same time. Don't need you getting your heads blown off by not looking around as you come." That said, he rode on ahead.

The patrol waited till Tye was well out of sight before following. Harrison commented.

"How does a man do that? I mean how a man can find within himself to put his self in obvious danger like Tye does and never show any emotion."

"I can tell you what Tye told me once about that. He said that when on patrol scouting he never feels more alive at that time. Same as going into a fight. As far as emotion goes I know you seen him in a fight with the Comanche, but you have never seen him really pissed. And if you do you had better pray it ain't you he is pissed at. That's all I'm gonna say about it except that ever man on the fort is glad he is on our side."

A little to the south of where Tye is tracking the outlaw gang Dan August scouting for the troops looking for Juh and his band rounded a hill and ran smack into the Apaches led by Juh. Dan and the Apache were both surprised. Dan reacted quickly, reining his mount around he was off back toward the patrol and away from the large band of warriors. Juh was quickly on his tail thinking it was just a cowboy and would be an easy kill.

Dan rode low in the saddle, his hat flapping on the back of his neck held by the chin strap. Looking over his shoulder he saw the Apache about two hundred yards behind him. He figured he was a mile from where patrol should be. A minute later he fired his colt in the air as fast as he could cock it and pull the trigger hoping to warn the patrol.

Bullis heard first of the shots and held up the patrol. When more shots followed he quickly called for the men to form a skirmish line and wait for his command. As they sat there Dan could be seen rushing toward them with a hell of lot of Apache hot on his tail. With no time to look for cover Bullis ordered his men to dismount, and every fourth man take horses with them and get the hell behind them. The remaining men lay on the ground with their recently acquired seven shot repeating Spencer, some scared to death feeling the earth shake from the pounding hooves and hearing the fierce Apache war cries. Dan arrived and slid his horse on the horse's rear end and jumped out of the saddle amidst all the dust after grabbing his Spencer from the saddle holster. "You wanted Juh so I brought him to you Sir," he hollered to Bullis as he laid down beside the officer.

"OPEN FIRE," Bullis shouted to his men. Rifles blasted from both sides of Bullis and Dan and several ponies suddenly had no riders.

The Apaches, surprised by the soldier's sudden appearance swerved to the right and retreated three or four hundred yards back the direction they come from.

Bullis, knowing the reason the Apache did not overrun them was because they were probably surprised at the presence of soldiers. They would come again, and he did not want to fight them in the open.

"Let's find a place we can defend," he said to Dan.

"My thinking also," Dan replied.

"Get your mounts and follow me," he shouted. Men scrambled to the horse holders and in less than a minute were mounted and following Bullis and Dan at a gallop.

Not being able to see behind them for the dust Dan hollered at Bullis that he was dropping back to see what the Apaches were doing. When he could see he saw the Apaches about a quarter of a mile behind them and coming fast. He raced his horse back up to where Bullis was and yelled, "Behind us three or four hundred yards."

Bullis nodded his understanding and pointed to the right with his Spencer to what appeared to be a huge buffalo wallow and headed toward it. Arriving both he and Dan was surprised that it was ten foot or so deep. Both men had their mounts to the bottom quickly with the troopers following. One could barely see for the dust, but Bullis shouted.

"Sargent Gregory, assign three men to watch the horses everyone else on the rim of the wallow and be ready to fight for your life." Twenty-four men scrambled to the rim where Bullis and Dan lay. The Apache were one hundred fifty yards away and charging fast.

"Say your prayers Lieutenant," Dan hollered.

Bullis hesitated a couple seconds and when the Apache were about seventy yards away he shouted, **"Fire at will!"** His, Dan's and twenty-four other rifles fired at once and a lot of riderless ponies were running with the others. The Apache swerved when they were almost on top of the soldiers and loosed their arrows as they rode by with some firing their repeaters and rode back about a quarter mile away to reassemble.

"Sergeant Gregory," Bullis shouted. "Get me a casualty report." It was quiet for a moment and then a voice said.

"Suh, Sergeant Gregory is dead Suh."

"Who is this?"

"Private Keene, Suh."

Bullis recognized the name as being one of his Seminole scouts that were with the troops."

"Yes Suh Lootenant Bullis."

Dammit to hell," Bullis muttered to Dan. "Gregory was my right hand man and one of the finest soldiers I have ever known. All the Seminole scouts under my command looked up to him.

He wa.... He stopped as Private Keene shouted, "Six dead and ten wounded six of which can still fight, Suh."

"Thank you Keene," Bullis said loud enough for him to hear. "Corporal Judson, can you hear me?"

"Corporal Judson is wounded pretty bad, Suh," Keene answered.

"Son-of-a-...," Bullis caught himself and didn't finish. "What do you think Dan?"

Dan looked out and in front of the wallow. "There's about twenty dead Apaches out there and probably a few more hurting pretty bad. He won't charge like that again."

"What do you think he will do?"

Dan looked up at the cloudless June sky and a sun that was almost to the mid-point of crossing the sky. "It's almost noon and going to be hot in a little while and going to be hotter than hell in this hole we are in. I think Juh will play a waiting game. He knows we have only the water in our canteens so he will see how we do when the water runs out. He looked left and right. I can't see a way out of here right now but I'm going to look around."

Bullis nodded. "All you men go easy on the water in your canteens and only take a swallow when you need to," he said loud enough for all to hear. "Saving the water may save your life."

A short way northwest of Bullis and the patrol, Tye squatted on his heels studying the tracks of the outlaws. He was unaware of the drama just southeast of where he was. He was concerned about his present situation and the danger it represented. He was looking at the boot prints of a man mingled in with the tracks of the outlaw's horse. They were fresh, probably less than thirty minutes. The tracks of the other horses were about an hour old so they had a man dropping back to look for a scout or posse following them. Knowing this sent a chill up his spine. Not because it scared him but knowing this and the fact he was in constant danger of an ambush made him feel alive. He decided to wait for the others.

Ten minutes later he heard the patrol coming, shod hooves striking rocks, sabers rattling, saddles squeaking, and men coughing every once in a while made him smile. It's a wonder we ever see an Apache because we sure as hell ain't going to sneak up on them. He showed Lieutenant Harrison the tracks. "See how the tracks of the horses are covered by the boot prints which means the man here was here after the others. They figure they are being followed and intend to set an ambush up."

"So, what do you suggest we do?"

"I need an extra pair of eyes with me out front to watch for exactly that."

Harrison stood up. He figured he needed Sergeant Bailey in case something happened to Tye. He knew he probably could not find his way back to Clark, well he probably he could, eventually. "Private Riley."

A few seconds later Private Riley was there and Saluting. "Yes Sir."

Harrison returned the salute. "Riley, I want you to ride with Tye and be an extra pair of eyes for him. He's expecting trouble."

"Yes Sir," Riley replied and after saluting again did a quick about face and mounting his horse and rode over to Tye.

Tye reached out and shook the man's hand and after explaining the situation they rode off ahead of the others.

Gary McMillan

Chapter Three

Juh, sitting cross legged Indian style, was in a discussion with his friends, Nantan, Kuruk, and Nana about how there were going to kill the white eyes. Kuruk, the most aggressive of the four, was for charging and over running them.

Juh nodded. "We could do that but how many more of our brothers would be killed. We have already lost many and many wives will be mourning their dead husbands and how many children would lose their fathers. No, we will wait and let the sun take the moisture from their bodies making them weak."

"That make take two moons or more," the warrior Kuruk argued.

"Do you have something to do today that cannot wait?" Juh asked raising his voice. "The soldiers will be just as dead in a day or so as they would be now and we still have all of our brothers. You know how crazy in the head," he said pointing to his own head, lack of water causes. When they are weak we will attack and not before.

"There's no way out that I could see Lieutenant," Dan said returning from looking behind them."

"Why haven't they attacked?" Bullis asked.

"Juh is smart Sir. He lost a good number of men earlier and doesn't want that to happen again. I think he will wait us out."

"What do you mean by that?"

"You ever see men that haven't had a drink of water in a day or so in this heat. They go sorter crazy. A man loses his common sense, sees things that are not there. This troop would be easy to wipe out if things go that far. I've seen it before."

"Then what the hell do you suggest we do?"

"Wait. Have one man gather the canteens and be responsible for dispersing the water out a little at a time to the men. I know men and they will drink when they don't really need to if you leave the water to them."

"Private Keene," he said loudly. When Keene came to him he said. Let each man take one swallow from their canteens the gather all of the canteens and you will disperse one swallow to each man when I say so. You sit with the wounded and use your own judgement as to when they need water.

Bullis turned to Dan. "We're in a hell of a fix aren't we?"

"We are at that Sir."

Tye, lying on his belly behind some thick junipers on top of a hill, looked down at the outlaws who were apparently resting themselves and their horses. The last time one of them had dropped behind was where Tye had seen their tracks about three hours ago and he figured they didn't think they were being followed and now were in no hurry. He had sent Riley back to get the patrol.

Fifteen minutes later Tye scooted back down the hill when he saw the patrol coming. He explained the situation and what he thought they should do. Harrison would stay on top of the hill with two men, Privates Riley and Reardon. Tye would take the others and dropped of Privates Riley and Reardon on the left side of the outlaws and moving behind the outlaws dropped off Sargent Arnold and Corporal Garner he would approach the gang from Harrison's left with Private Williams. A neat trap. Harrison agreed and taking his campaign hat off as well as the others, crawled to the top to settle themselves behind the junipers and wait for Tye to make his move.

Twenty minutes later Tye had everyone in position, and he instructed Williams to stay hidden but have his rifle ready. Tye stood up and was immediately spotted by the camp and all pulled their guns

"Who the hell are you and what do you want?" Yelled Isaac.

"Smelled your coffee and thought I might get a cup from you. Been a while since I had any," Tye answered smiling with his hands out away from his Colt.

"What in damnation are you doing out here?" Billy asked.

"Looking for some men that killed some people back in Brackett," Tye replied still smiling but turned his body slightly so his Colt could not be seen. "Thought you men might have some seen five men riding out here."

On the hill above, Harrison could hear every word and wondered what the hell Tye was doing. To his left Private Reardon chuckled.

"What's so funny Private?"

"Sorry Sir," Reardon said and added. "Tye won't shoot a man in the back nor from ambush unless there is no other way. He knows what he is doing, and those men have no idea how fast he can draw and shoot."

"We haven't seen anyone so get the hell away from our camp," Isaac shouted.

"Well now, that's not very neighborly of you but you might look around. You are surrounded by a patrol from Fort Clark." The men looked around and saw no one.

"Who are you?" Isaac asked.

"Tye Watkins, scout out of Fort Clark. Drop your guns and no one gets hurt."

"Like hell we will," Billy said and swung his gun toward Tye and died immediately as Tye's Colt suddenly appeared in his hand and belched lead and smoke. Harrison and the others opened up as the outlaws scrambled for cover. Buck James was a little slow and was shot by Bailey and Garner. Tye had fired his Colt that killed Billy and threw himself to the side just as bullets cut the air where he had stood. He fired again and hit Rufus in the shoulder as the outlaw scrambled for cover. Isaac lay behind some boulders as bullets splattered and ricochet all around him with rock fragments cutting his face but missing his eyes. Rufus lay on the ground a few feet from him moaning and holding his shattered right shoulder.

He looked over at his brother, Billy, who lay where he fell and never moved. "You bastard Watkins I'm gonna kill you if it's the last thing I ever do."

"You ain't the first outlaw who said that," Arnold said. The remark brought laughter from the others which infuriated Isaac who fired his pistol in the direction of Arnold's voice. A round of fire from all the soldiers splattered him with more rock fragments.

"Don't shoot anymore," he shouted and threw his Colt out on the ground. He stood up and stepped from behind the boulder he was behind. He was quickly surrounded. As Arnold grabbed his arms and pulled them roughly behind his back he shouted at Watkins.

"So you are the great scout that has everyone including the Apache scared of. You sure as hell don't look like much to me and if all these damn soldiers weren't here I'd kick your sorry ass from here to yonder." Isaac was almost as big as Tye and didn't appear to have any fat on him.

Arnold looked at Tye and Tye nodded. Arnold released his grip on the outlaw's wrist and shoved him toward Tye.

"What are you doing Arnold?" Harrison asked.

"Fixing to watch the fun Sir. This worthless piece of shit needs a little lesson."

Isaac looked all around kind of befuddled he had been released.

"Go ahead and kick his ass," Corporal Garner said laughing. Harrison was at a loss. They just released a man who had killed a lot of people.

Arnold looked at Harrison. "Don't worry Lieutenant, he is just gonna get a little lesson."

Tye stepped up to Isaac after taking his Colts and Bowie and handing them to a befuddled Harrison.

"Take your best shot. These soldiers are not going to interfere," Tye said. Isaac looked at his brother who lay on his back, his open lifeless eyes.

"You Son-of-a-Bitch," he screamed as he unleashed a right towards Tye's jaw. Tye ducked under the roundhouse right and planted a hard right of his own in the outlaw's belly. Isaac doubled over and his face met Tye's knee which was coming up. The soldiers all winced at the sound of a busted nose and probably some loose teeth.

He fell to the ground and lay in the fetal position gasping for air. Tye reached down and jerked the man to his feet. "You can get some air in your lungs standing up better than you can lying on the ground moaning like a baby.

Isaac stood there sucking in air and wiping the blood from his busted nose off with his shirt sleeve, He stood there swaying some trying to decide what to do. He wasn't as confident as he was a minute ago. He had been in a lot of fights and never lost then again he had never been hit that hard either.

"Well, I'm waiting," Tye said. With that said Isaac feinted with his right and followed with a left that clipped Tye on the cheek as he ducked. Then Isaac got a lesson. He got hit with a right on the left cheek bone followed by a left to this nose. Both licks came so fast they seemed almost to come at the same time. He staggered back but then caught another right where he lived, and it was all over as he crumbled once again to the ground gasping.

"Another 'bad dude' gets a lesson," Arnold said laughing along with the others. Even Harrison had to smile.

Harrison told Arnold to tie the man's hands and get him on a horse along with the wounded man. The other men gathered up all the weapons and then wrapped Billy in a ground cloth and tied him across a saddle.

Harrison gave Tye his Colt and Bowie back. "That was entertaining."

Tye, taking his weapons back smiled and said. "Seems every bad dude I ever brought in thinks he is toughest man in the world. They just have to be taught different."

"Well, he certainly learned a lesson," the lieutenant said looking at a slumping, moaning Isaac. Rufus, who had been watching, thought, *maybe next time Isaac would listen to him, if there was a next time*

It was mid-morning as they headed east toward Clark.

The Apache had the same problem as all Indians when it came to fighting the soldiers: lack of discipline. All tribes had their war chiefs, but the Indian did as he wanted. This lack of discipline was the downfall of many battles lost that could have been won by the Redman. Juh's friend Kuruk was to be an example of this. He was a great warrior and had several followers even in Juh's camp. He gathered them together and before Juh could stop them they charged the soldiers in the wallow. They were thirty or so with Kuruk. Juh, disgusted with his friend knew they would be slaughtered by the soldiers' rifles let out a war cry and all the rest along with him charged right behind Kuruk and his men.

The charge caught the soldiers napping and the Apache were less than one hundred yards away before Harrison and Dan got them to the rim and firing their rifles. This time however, at fifty yards the Apache leaped from their mounts and zigzagged a path toward the soldiers making themselves a much harder target to hit.

Arrows and lances were released by the warriors and who then charged with knives and war clubs. One could not hardly see for the smoke from the rifles and the men could only hear war cries and the sounds of men screaming. The soldier next to Bullis took a ten-foot war lance in the chest with the point protruding three feet out his back. Dan had an arrow in his left shoulder but was still firing his colt. He knew things were bad and going to get a lot worse as an Apache leaped at him with a knife. Bullis who was firing his Colt with his right hand shot the warrior at point blank range in the chest. The impact of the forty-five slugs knocked the brave back over the rim and on his back and didn't move. Another Apache came at him, and he stroked the trigger of his Colt, but the hammer fell on an empty chamber. The lieutenant dropped his pistol and grabbed his saber and managed to get it pointed at the Apache just as the man leaped at him. The point of the blade entered his belly and went clean thru to the hilt. The warrior and Bullis looked each other in the eye. The warrior had an astonished look on his face, then died.

Bullis put his boot on the dead Apache's chest and ripped his saber from his belly. He looked to his left and saw Dan on his back with two Apache on top of him. Dan drove in knife in one their chest and the lieutenant's saber almost beheaded the other showering Dan with blood.

They both knew all was lost as more soldiers were dead or dying in the wallow.

A few minutes earlier Tye had heard the rifle fire. "What the hell?" Tye shouted as he halted the patrol. "Someone is in a lot of trouble Lieutenant just over that hill. Stay here Sir," he said and rode the fifty yards to the crest of the hill dismounting just before he topped it so as not to skyline himself. "Damn!" he muttered to himself and remounted and headed back down the hill as he saw the Apache almost to the soldiers in the wallow.

"Arnold," he hollered. "You still have that old bugle in your saddle bags?"

"Yes Sir."

"Get ready to blow charge as best you can." Tye leaped from his horse and began cutting mesquite limbs and tying a rope to them. He handed the rope to Bailey. "When Arnold blows that bugle ya'll follow me and you drag that brush Arnold." He remounted Sandy. "Blow the damn bugle Arnold and he kneed Sandy into a run with everyone following except Garner. He stayed with the prisoners.

Tye led the little group around the hill with Arnold blowing the worst charge tune he had ever heard. He was firing his Colt in the air just to get the Apache's attention. It was not necessary as the Apache had heard the bugle. With all the dust behind the first row of bluecoats they could not tell how many there were. They made a quick disappearing act like only the Apache can.

Tye and the others had their mounts on their haunches sliding to a stop in a cloud of dust.

Bullis jumped out of the wallow his head bleeding and grabbed Tye's hand and then Harrison's. "Don't know where you come from but you wasn't a minute to early. We were done for."

"We can talk later Lieutenant," Tye said. "It's not going to take the Apache long to figure out they were tricked so get your dead and wounded and everyone on a horse and let's get the hell out of here and find a better place to defend if need be." Less than ten minutes later they picked up Garner and the prisoners and galloping toward the fort.

Chapter Four

Tye led the patrol northeast for several miles before halting. They had trotted, galloped, and walked the horses for over three hours. Tye found a place they could defend better than the wallow the patrol had been in. He wanted to rest and then head out again, but he had to think of the wounded. They were still about twenty miles from Clark as the crow flies but farther the way they had to travel. They were among some huge boulders with a forty-foot cliff behind them. It was not the best location to defend because of ricochets from the rocks. They can cause some horrific wounds but under the circumstances it would have to do. As soon as everyone was settled in the boulders Tye started looking to the wounded. Most of the injuries were arrows in various parts of the body but two had pretty bad head wounds probably from a glancing blow from a war club.

Tye had two men he knew had some experience with arrow wounds helping him. Lieutenant Bullis was beside Tye helping him remove arrows and close the wounds with a hot knife after an antiseptic was poured into the wound. The antiseptic was rot gut whiskey which more than burned a little but not near like the hot knife that melted the flesh over the hole. One hour later Tye was through and he and Bullis along with Harrison squatted around a small fire sipping coffee.

Bullis asked Tye. "Do you really think Juh will follow us?"

Tye answered. "Lieutenant, the Apache warrior is a proud man. Nothing means more to him than his honor and reputation. We have hurt Juh where it hurts the most, his reputation as the best war chief of the Janeros band of Chiricahua Apache. He is normally in Arizona, but he sometimes comes to Mexico along the Texas Border looking to kill Mexicans and take their children and women. If things are not going good as far as killing Mexicans he will cross the Rio Grande into Texas. To answer your question, yes I think he will hit us pretty damn quick."

Sergeant Arnold approached Tye, Bullis and Harrison walking briskly. "Look over yonder on the hill," he said pointing south.

"Damn!" Tye said loudly.

"What does that mean?" Harrison asked as all looked at the smoke signals Arnold had pointed out.

"Three puffs repeated over and over could mean Juh is calling for help," Tye said. "Apache use smoke signals like the other tribes but can have different meanings to each tribe. Three quick puffs used repeatedly usually is a call for help or come to me in Apache smoke. Juh is calling other Apache to come to him quickly." Both Lieutenants stared at Tye so Tye said. "If he gets more warriors we are as good as dead if we stay here. We need to tie the dead securely to the saddles and have the wounded that cannot stay in the saddle strapped behind a healthy trooper. We need to be ready to leave as soon as it gets dark." He looked at the sun and said it's about six thirty or so now so let's get to it and be ready at dark." Harrison looked at his pocket watch and smiled despite the situation: Six forty-two.

Clouds rolled in just before dusk and it made Tye feel better. He would be happier if it rained with lots of thunder to help cover their noise when leaving. He was with both lieutenants and Sergeant Arnold. "It's almost full dark so get ready to pull out. If Juh had more Apache come to him I figure he will already have some warriors between us and the fort with the main bunch ready to hit us at the boulders at daybreak. Tell your men if we run into some Apache do not stop. We will charge and fight our way through them. If any man stops, he's as good as dead. Give the wounded that is strapped behind a trooper a side arm that is fully loaded. If we meet them, stay low and run like the devil is chasing you and shoot anything that is not going your direction."

Fifteen minutes later the troops were behind Tye, Dan and the two lieutenants in a rough skirmish line. They moved out at a walk with no talking or unnecessary noise. Dan and Arnold then moved over to be with some of the men that were to Tye's and the lieutenants left and right to make sure they did as Tye said if trouble came. Thirty minutes later they came upon the Apache sudden like. The Apache charged the troops whooping and screaming their insults. There, in Tye's quick guess about forty of them which may not to most seem like a lot but these are Apache which makes a huge difference.

"Let's go," Tye said turning in the saddle to Bullis and Harrison.

Both lieutenants screamed at the same time, **"CHARGE!"**

A few seconds later every man was fighting for his life. Apache were leaping from their pony's back trying to knock a soldier from his saddle. They were releasing their arrows with deadly accuracy. One soldier with a wounded man tied behind him had an arrow in the shoulder and another in the chest but stayed in the saddle with the wounded man behind him firing his pistol unaware the man was fatally wounded. Soldiers' horses when down with arrows in them and the men were instantly pounced on by an Apache or more than one Apache. The men were stabbed and clubbed to death within seconds of hitting the ground.

Tye broke through the charging Apache and turned around just in time to see Harrison's horse go down throwing the lieutenant. Harrison had seen the arrow strike his horse in the chest seconds before and took his boots from the stirrups. When the horse stumbled he leapt from the saddle and landed on his feet but with the speed that the horse was running he could only take two giant steps before hitting the ground hard stunning him. Tye saw this and cursing, reined Sandy around to help him. Bullis seeing Tye doing this did the same and immediately saw the problem. Tye shot one

Apache that was already standing over Harrison who had raised up on his elbows shaking his head trying to get his bearings. Tye's forty-five caliber slug caught the warrior in the chest just as the man was raising his butcher knife to stab the lieutenant in the back. Tye heard the crack of a pistol and felt the bullet cutting the air close to his head. He saw another Apache thrown backwards as the brave ran to finish off Harrison. Tye glanced over his shoulder and smiled when he saw Bullis behind him and it was he who had fired the shot.

Other troops had their hands full. Some trying to fight off an Apache who leaped up behind the troopers and doing their damndest to get the bluecoats off their horse and on the ground. Tye leaped off Sandy grabbing Harrison by the collar and the back of his pants threw him on Sandy. He leaped on behind the saddle and holding Harrison he kicked Sandy into a gallop with Bullis following. Looking over his shoulder he saw most of the men were following but he could tell they were a hell of a lot fewer than before they ran into the warriors

Arnold was riding beside Bullis when an Apache leaped from his pony onto the back of the sergeant. Arnold didn't panic like most of the men had and taking his Colt reached around his belly and pulled the trigger. The Apache was blown off Arnold's horse and was dead before he hit the rocky ground. Arnold's side burned like hell from the flash of the powder when he pulled the trigger, but he was alive.

The Apache fell behind what was left of the troops. Tye knew why: they would kill the troopers who had been knocked off their mounts after torturing any trooper who was unfortunate enough to still be alive. They would scalp and mutilate them after they were dead and celebrate what they considered a victory.

Tye slowed the horses to a fast walk. They were less than twenty miles from the fort, but the men and horses were worn out. They needed to rest up, but the problem was Juh. He would be on their trail as soon as he gathered up all the warriors who had come to join him. He knew of an abandoned homestead a mile or so from where they were. It was well built with thick sod walls and a roof that had several inches of grass and sod on top of it making it pretty much fireproof. If he remembered correctly there was a large barn just a stone throw from the home that could be defended and would hold most of their horses if not all. He had spent a lot of time there with his friends before the Apache Tanza and his bunch raided and killed the whole family.

Guiding the troops unerringly through the darkness he found the homestead twenty minutes later. Both lieutenants and Tye along with ten soldiers settled in the homestead with the wounded and the rest and the horses were in the barn with Sergeant Arnold. Tye made a quick round of the wounded speaking with each man and giving words of encouragement even though he knew some were beyond saving. He spoke to Bullis and Harrison.

"We are no more than twenty miles from Clark. Some of the wounded will die for sure if we try to move them again and even if we do head to Clark, Juh will overtake us because of how slow we will be traveling."

"So, what do you suggest we do?" Bullis asked.

"Been asking myself the same question Lieutenant and the only thing I know to do is fort up here the best we can. We can send Arnold to Clark and if things go okay he could be back with help by mid-morning or maybe a little sooner. We'll just have to hold out till then. These walls are two foot thick, and the roof is covered in sod so being burned out is not likely. You two stay here and I will go to the barn with the other men."

Bullis spoke to a private telling him to go get Arnold. Harrison told two other men to get buckets and fill them with water from the well and fill everything in the homestead that will hold water. Tye figured the lieutenants had things under control so as he left he spoke to both men.

"I am going to have my men hold their fire until the Apache are almost on you. When we open up they will find themselves in a serious crossfire." Both men nodded their understanding. "I figure since the Apache like most tribes don't like to fight at night, they will be on us at first light."

"Those damn Apache sure fought like maniacs a little while ago and it was almost dark," Harrison.

"We surprised them Lieutenant."

On his way he met the private coming back with Arnold. "We are depending on you Arnold to get help back as fast as possible. Take three horses and switch back and forth riding between them. Good luck," he said shaking the sergeant's hand.

"I'll be back Tye. You can count on it. He didn't get far as he came riding back like the devil was chasing him. It wasn't the devil but about fifteen Apache.

The men settled in for the night. Since the Apache knew where they were they made a small fire in the barn and made coffee: Soldiers coffee, hot, black and strong. Tye made a count of heads. Twelve men and each had his seven shot Spencer. Tye had his thirteen shot Henry so they could muster a lot of firepower. Full dark settled around them. Tye set up a watch schedule of two men at a time on two-hour shifts. He was going to take the last, just before dawn.

Bullis and Harrison did likewise: head count and made coffee. They had nine healthy men and three, maybe four of the wounded that could handle a rifle making a total of fifteen counting themselves. Not a good number against maybe sixty or so Apache and maybe even more by now if more showed up. They all drank some coffee and tried to get some sleep.

Chapter Five

Dawn came with pounding hooves and screaming Apache war cries. Arrows were hitting the homestead with some finding their way through windows. Two men went down before Bullis gave the order to fire. Several ponies were without riders after the first volley and for some reason, known only to an Apache, they swerved away and retreated back to where they were before the attack. The men shouted their excitement when seeing this. Tye hollered over to them.

"Don't get excited yet. They were just testing us and will be back after Juh forms a plan. I suggest you put a couple or three men watching the backside of the homestead. They will probably come from all directions."

Bullis shouted back. "We lost two men in that attack. I don't think Juh knows how thin we are in the ranks."

"Probably true Lieutenant," Tye shouted back. "His main bunch will hit you head on and couple smaller groups from the back and your left side. He will figure to draw some of your fire power away from the front but then that's when we will surprise him."

The men in the barn had placed some old bales of hay in the doorway of the barn to lay behind and men manned both windows in the loft. Ten minutes later they came again and as Tye predicted. From the front, back and one side. Arrows were flying through the windows as thick as flies on horse dung and some were striking flesh. The soldiers opened up and several bucks hit the hard ground, but the soldiers were under manned in the rear and that's where the problem reared its ugly head.

The Apache attacking the front were within twenty yards of the door when Tye and his men opened up from the barn. All though caught by surprise the Apache quickly swerved toward the barn and some made it through the open barn door their ponies jumping the stacked bales of hay. It was no problem for the Apache to fire down on the troops as they raced through the open door as they had been taught since childhood to ride and fire their arrows accurately from a jumping or running horse.

The men in the home had their own problems as they were fighting hand to hand with the Apache who had overwhelmed the two men in the rear window and were climbing through the window. Both lieutenants and the other four men found themselves fighting for their lives with eight or ten warriors who had come in through the window. Bullis figured all was lost.

Tye shouted to the men in the loft to get over to the edge and fire down on the warriors attacking the men on the ground floor. Tye grabbing his Bowie and tomahawk leaped from the loft to the floor, hit the floor and somersaulting to his feet and began slashing right and left at everything that was not blue and he begin screaming like a banshee. Between his killing with the tomahawk and Bowie and the men in the loft's deadly fire and their following Tye's lead screaming their lungs out the few remaining Apache braves scrambled out of the barn and away from these crazy bluecoats especially the big one in deerskin clothes with the knife and tomahawk.

Tye seeing all the braves had left the barn hollered to the men, "follow me," and rushed to the homestead bursting through the door and immediately was attacked by two Apache. He killed one with his tomahawk busting the man's head open. The other brave droved his knife deep into Tye's left shoulder while Tye was occupied with the one he had hit in the head with his tomahawk. Full of adrenaline, Tye jerked the brave's hand away from the handle and slashing down with the tomahawk that was in his right hand split the man's skull splattering bone fragments and brain matter over him and anyone else that was close. He cut loose with another of his famous animal screams that could be heard over the noise of battle in the room.

At that time the remaining four troopers who had followed Tye burst through the door and that proved too much for the Apache who scrambled out the rear window and then were shot in the back by troopers who had ran to the window and fired at the fleeing warriors.

Tye looked around and was appalled at the sight. Bodies, both troopers and Apache, lay everywhere and the one could not take a step without stepping in the blood and gore. He spotted Bullis sitting against the front wall, an arrow in his shoulder. Harrison lay with a knife protruding from his back and his sword in the chest of an Apache. Tye rolled him over and a low groan came from his throat.

"God, he's still alive," Tye mumbled and taking a closer look saw the knife was high in his back and just under the right collar bone. "Maybe it missed his lungs," Tye said hopefully looking at the angle of the knife which was away from his heart and lungs. He had grown to like this young man and had hopes of him becoming a good officer.

Tye hollered at the remaining men to get to the windows in case of another attack. He scrambled around looking to the wounded ignoring the pain in his left shoulder which still had the Apache knife in it to the amazement of the soldiers. After doing what he could for the wounded he removed the arrow from Bullis and cauterized it with a hot blade. He then sat with his back against the wall where Bullis was and passed out. His friend and fellow scout Dan August rushed over despite an arrow that Tye had removed from his right thigh. Despite the pain in his leg, he sat on the floor and cradled Tye's head in his lap.

"Dammit!" he shouted. "Someone get me something to stuff in this wound before he bleeds to death" Men who appreciated Tye's unselfishness in caring for them and their friends despite his wound rushed over ripping their blue tunics off and cutting strips from the shirt of their long johns.

Dan was glad his friend had passed out because jerking the knife out was going to hurt. When he did a low groan came from Tye's lips and the blood flowed even more. He managed to stem it to a trickle pressing down the strips of shirts. He knew this not very sanitary but if he did not stop the blood Tye was a dead man.

"Any Apache out there," he hollered to the men at the windows and door?"

"No sir," came from three or four throats. "Then one of you run to the barn and find my horse and get the bottle of rot gut from the left saddle bag. One of you stir that fire up and put this in it," he said sliding his knife across the floor to one of the men.

A few minutes later the knife was glowing red. He removed the wad of bloody shirt from the cut and poured the whiskey on the wound resulting in more low groans from Tye. He then slid the blade across the cut and melted the flesh together. More groans, a little louder this time. A trooper brought his folded tunic over and Dan removed Tye's head from his lap and lay it on the tunic. Bullis led the men in a prayer which was followed with a loud AMEN.

Lt. Harrison, lying on the floor with his head propped on his tunic, noticed that every man, wounded and unwounded, was also praying along with Bullis. *This man,* he thought to himself, *this man is loved even more than I thought. These troopers, mostly drifters, ex-buffalo hunters, and even outlaws joining the army to escape the law were not men to show emotion, but these were. They truly loved that man,* he mumbled to himself. *I've only been around him for a few weeks, but I can understand now why they do. Not only does he fight like a demon, but he cares for the men as was shown by his helping the wounded here until he passed out from loss of blood despite being told by Bullis, Dan and others to take care of himself. The men had probably seen this before and greatly appreciated his feeling for them.*

Bullis had Dan ride to the fort with an extra horse to get the surgeon and a hospital wagon headed back toward them. He was afraid moving not only Tye but two of the more seriously wounded men would not survive the jostling around on a travois. Beds could be made in the wagon plus they all needed professional medical attention. *We'll wait and hope the Apache doesn't come back*, he thought.

Dan arrived at the fort just before dark. After explaining the situation to Major Thurston, the major ordered one of his orderlies to get Master Sargent O'Malley right away. When O'Malley arrived, Thurston told him to get a thirty-man patrol together and also the surgeon and a wagon.

"Yes Sir," O'Malley replied. "If you don't mind me asking sir, what's going on?"

The patrols with Bullis and Harrison combined forces but were attacked repeatedly by Juh and about one hundred of his braves. They are holed up in a homestead and most are dead or wounded with Tye being one of the more serious. We are going to them now.

"Tye wounded," he said and turned and ran out the door. He reached the enlisted men's barracks and shouted, "I need thirty men for a rescue patrol. Tye and several men are hurt badly, and several are dead. He could have had fifty men if he wanted them as at least that many jumped up. He hollered names of those he knew had been around awhile and then rushed to his quarters to tell his wife what was going on.

"Oh God!" She exclaimed. She helped her man get his things together and as he left she told him she loved him. He came back and hugged her.

When he was gone she rushed to Tye's home to tell Rebecca. Buff answered the door. When told, Rebecca hugged her and began sobbing. Buff rushed over and pulled her away from Mrs. O'Malley and hugged her.

"Rebecca," he whispered, "How manee times has Tye been hurt and has always cumm back ta yu and the kids. He has dun tole yu over and over he will cumm back ta yu and he will this time."

Rebecca stopped sobbing and pulled back from Buff. "You old coot, you always know what to say. The kids and me love you so much." She added after wiping the tears away and stood up straight. "You are right Buff; he will come back. Thank you."

At headquarters the patrol was forming up. The post surgeon was in his wagon with an assistant and a full load of medical supplies. Everyone was surprised when Major Thurston mounted a horse and led the patrol out of Fort Clark. It was ten P.M.. With the wagon slowing them down it would be daylight or shortly after when they reached the homestead Dan was leading them to. They didn't know just how critical their arriving would be.

Chapter Six

Tye was slowly coming awake about the time the patrol was leaving Clark. Bullis was beside him and wiped his forehead and face with a wet kerchief.

"Welcome back to the land of the living Tye. You gave all of us a scare." When the word spread around the homestead that Tye was coming to a loud HIP HIP HURRAY was heard from the troops and then repeated.

Tye looked around and asked Bullis. "How long have I been out Lieutenant?"

"Several hours Tye. I sent Dan to Clark to get the doctor and extra troops. I was afraid you and some of the wounded troops would not make the trip without some medical help,"

Tye nodded and asked. "Any Apache shown up since the fight?" Bullis shook his head. "Well, we had better be ready come daybreak. We've beaten him twice and he ain't going to forget it. He'll hit us hard come daybreak. I'll stake my reputation om it."

"Good God," exclaimed Bullis. "I've only got six or seven healthy men."

"I know that so if I may make a suggestion you need to put at least two healthy men at the windows and door. Have the wounded that can help be by them and keep their Spencer's loaded. Each healthy man has their rifle and one of the wounded men's guns. I hope I am wrong, but it thinks it's gonna get real nasty."

"I'll get the men together and tell them what you said. After that I'll assign them each to a window or door and the wounded that can help also." Tye nodded and drank some more water and lay back to relax.

About two in the morning Tye woke up and surprised himself that he felt much better, much stronger than just four or so hours ago. His shoulder hurt like hell, but he could deal with that if he wasn't pretty helpless like he was earlier. He drank more water and slowly stood up. He was dizzy for a couple of seconds, but it quickly passed.

He walked over to where Sargent Arnold was at a window.

"Damn, Tye, it's sure good to see you up and around. I know the men will be glad to see you also. It will give them a little hope."

Tye nodded and spoke. "I'll be around when it gets nasty." He walked slowly to the other window and then to the door speaking to each of the men that were watching and being careful not to wake those that were not.

Daylight came with the sound the men had heard before. Hooves of many ponies pounding the ground and Apache war cries ending the quiet and peacefulness of the early dawn. Arrows and an occasional bullet slammed into the walls of the homestead and thru the window. Bullis gave the order to fire and the morning air was filled with the sound of Spencer's firing from the window and door. The men heard the footsteps on the roof.

Tye rushed to the fireplace and put out the small fire. Tye rushed back to where Bullis was firing from the door. "They were going to plug up the Chimney to smoke us out."

Bullis nodded his understanding and said, "We may have to leave anyway with all the smoke from these damn rifles."

"Better to be a little uncomfortable in here than dead out there." A gasp from the window caused Tye to look that way only to see a trooper grasping an arrow that was in his throat. He hit the floor and gasped a couple times spraying blood from his lips and died. Tye rushed over to take his place and firing his Colt since his left hand was pretty useless as far as holding a rifle barrel.

Thru the smoke Tye saw Juh for a second and threw down on him firing a couple shots. He was surprised when he saw Juh slump forward over his pony's neck holding his shoulder. It was now becoming almost impossible to see in the smoke-filled room from the black powder shells. An Apache stuck his head and shoulders threw the window preparing to jump into the room. His head was crushed from the two and half pound Colt Tye hit him with.

Another trooper took Tye's place while Tye reloaded his Colt. Reloaded, Tye stepped back to the window just as the trooper who had taken his place killed an Apache with his knife. He looked at Tye and nodded his head obviously happy he had killed his first Apache with a knife.

Bullis was busy at the door trying to keep from being overrun. Two dead troopers with arrows in their chest lay at his feet. He was firing his Colt as fast as he could. A wounded trooper sat with his back to the wall reloading the lieutenants Colt and two others from dead troopers keeping Bullis with loaded guns. Dead

Apache were stacked up at the door dead from Bullis bullets as well as another trooper.

"That's all the bullets Sir," the wounded trooper yelled at Bullis as he handed him a Colt. The lieutenant fired and killed another Apache and of a sudden there was no more trying to get in to the amazement of the men still alive in the homestead. All was lost and now the fight was over, and a dead silence lay over the land. Then the men heard it. The greatest sound of all, a cavalry bugle sounding CHARGE!

A few seconds later blue clad soldiers filled the yard in front of the beleaguered homestead. Bullis and Tye shoved their way out the door thru the dead Apaches. They met Dan with both men hugging him. Then to both men's amazement, they saw Major Thurston walking toward them a smile as big as Texas across his face.

"Glad to see you two are still with us." Thurston looked at all the dead Apache. "My God, this is worse than I expected."

"Wait till you see inside Sir," Bullis said.

They stepped inside and the smell of gun smoke, blood, and of death hit Thurston hard.

"God Almighty," he mumbled. "I had forgotten how things smelled after a fight." He walked to where Lieutenant Harrison lay. "How are you doing Lieutenant," he asked while shaking Harrison's hand.

"Better than I would have if ya'll had been a few minutes later."

Thurston nodded and made the rounds shaking each man's hand, both the healthy and the wounded.

Sargent Arnold said as he shook the major's hand. "Thanks for rushing here Sir."

"You can thank Dan for getting us here." He motioned for Tye and Bullis to follow him outside. Taking a deep breath of fresh air he said. "What's the finale report?

"All told from the last two days we have twelve dead, fifteen wounded and three uninjured troopers Sir not counting Lieutenant Harrison and Tye."

"If you had been three or four minutes later Major it would be all dead, no survivors."

Thurston shook his head. "Thank God for that." Tye excused himself and went back inside the homestead.

"I need to tell you something Sir that you already know about that man," Bullis said nodding toward Tye. "When I went down with this a couple days ago," he pointed to the bandage on his head, "I was out for a few minutes and when I come to Tye was standing above me killing Apaches and keeping them off me. Then when he was wounded yesterday he helped with the wounded till he passed out from loss of blood. He is a remarkable man Sir."

"All of us at Clark know that Lieutenant. What you said does not surprise me one bit nor would it any other man at Clark. I can't imagine how bad the Apache and Comanche situation would be in this country without him."

It was noon when the troops headed back to Clark. Dan had ridden ahead to the fort to get the hospital staff ready for the wounded and dead and of course to tell his friends wife he was okay and would be in about dark.

It was a great reunion when Tye arrived at the fort as Rebecca leaped into his arms, much to the pain in his shoulder it caused. Rebecca, tears flowing, hugged and kissed him much to the delight of the troops. Seeing the kids, Tye dropped to his knees and hugged them with his good arm.

Rebecca, wiping the tears away said," Oh Tye, I was so scared when Mrs. O'Malley came and said you were hurt." He stood up when he heard the familiar weird words being spoken.

"I done tol Rebecca not ta wury her self nun that yu wur to sturbin ta die," Buff said. Tye hugged the little man. They went to the hospital so Tye could get his bandages changed then they went home so Rebecca could 'care' for him properly.

Everything was great for two weeks with Tye being home again and being with Rebecca, Buff, and the kids. He was teaching Little Ben how to read tracks when he learned that Buff had been doing it for the last few months. Little Ben could tell him the difference between, and buck deer and a doe's tracks. He could tell the difference between a coon track and a beaver track plus many more. *Old man is doing a great job as a grandpa*, he chuckled to himself.

The third week Tye was summoned to Thurston's office.

"Tye, I just received a dispatch from Grierson, the post commander Fort Concho." He handed it to Tye to read.

Major James Thurston

Post Commander of Ft Clark

There is a band of outlaws that may be headed your way. They number twenty to twenty-five and have already killed several homesteaders in our area. They are led by a man named Jason Billingsley and are ruthless leaving no one alive at the homesteads, man, woman or child. He is identified by being six foot five and wears a black eye patch over his left eye. Be on the look- out for them.

Colonel Grierson

Fort Concho

"What do you want to do Sir?" Tye asked.

"I want you to lead a patrol and Dan to lead a patrol north of here to warn settlers and to look for sign of these cutthroats. I want you to leave within the hour. I already have the quartermaster getting supplies together."

"Yes Sir," Tye said and thought to himself, *so much for peace and quiet*. He headed toward home to get ready to leave and start another chapter in the life of being a scout on the Border of Texas and Mexico.

Gary McMillan

www.ingramcontent.com/pod-product-compliance
Lightning Source LLC
Chambersburg PA
CBHW020637260626
47157CB00008B/2789